The
CONFIDENT
WARRIOR

How to Cultivate Confidence in Every Aspect of Your Life, then use it!

Table of Contents

About the Author

Kevin has overcome immense health challenges starting as a teenager when he underwent major surgery. In the years that followed, he endured numerous medical procedures and grappled with serious conditions. Through infections, rehabilitation, and complications, Kevin refused to view himself as a victim.

A key part of Kevin's resilience was cultivating an unshakable confidence that he could regain his health. During his darkest moments of fear and doubt, Kevin consciously fostered belief in his own inner strength. He focused his mind on visualizing a positive outcome, against all odds.

Practicing affirmations, prayer, and meditation, Kevin nurtured a quiet confidence that he would recover, even when medical facts said otherwise. This confidence gave him the courage to take difficult steps - to walk, exercise, work through pain. Kevin found energy and motivation from his belief in his ability to heal.

Slowly but surely, step by step, Kevin drew on his self-confidence to regain mobility and independence. Now he wants others to know that we all have vast wells of inner strength and self-belief that we can draw upon. Grim times can connect us with our deepest wisdom, resilience and confidence.

Kevin authored a book recounting his health journeys, highlighting the mind techniques he used. He shares how he conditioned his mindset, emotions and outlook through positive affirmations and visualizations. By committing to personal growth in the toughest of trials, we can unlock our greatest confidence. Kevin hopes his book will inspire confidence in anyone facing life's hardest battles.

Chapter 1: Understanding Fear and Confidence

Confidence is a complex and multifaceted trait that can have a profound impact on every aspect of our lives. It is the belief in oneself and one's abilities to achieve success, overcome challenges, and navigate through life's difficulties with grace and resilience.

Confidence is not just about having a positive self-image or feeling good about yourself; it is about having the inner strength and self-assurance to take risks, pursue your passions, and reach your full potential.

At its core, confidence is rooted in self-belief. It is the unwavering faith in your own abilities, judgment, and worth as a person. When you have self-belief, you trust in yourself to make the right decisions, even in the face of uncertainty or adversity. You know that you have the skills, knowledge, and resources to handle whatever comes your way, and you are not afraid to take on new challenges or step out of your comfort zone.

Self-confidence, on the other hand, is the outward manifestation of self-belief. It is the way you carry yourself, the way you interact with others, and the way you present yourself to the world. When you have self-confidence, you exude a sense of self-assurance and poise that is attractive and magnetic to others.

You speak with conviction, you stand tall, and you project an air of authority and competence.

Self-esteem is another key component of confidence. It is the way you feel about yourself, your worth, and your value as a person. When you have high self-esteem, you have a positive self-image and a healthy sense of self-worth. You know that you are deserving of love, respect, and success, and you are not afraid to go after what you want in life.

Confidence is not something that is innate or fixed. It is a skill that can be cultivated and developed over time through practice, self-awareness, and self-acceptance. It is about being comfortable in your own skin, embracing your strengths and weaknesses, and trusting in your own judgment.

One of the key ways to build confidence is to set realistic goals and work towards them consistently. When you set goals that are challenging but achievable, you give yourself the opportunity to experience success and build momentum. Each small victory builds upon the last, creating a positive feedback loop that reinforces your self-belief and self-confidence.

Another important aspect of building confidence is to surround yourself with positive and supportive people. When you are surrounded by people who believe in you and support your goals and dreams, you are more likely to feel confident and empowered. Seek out mentors, friends, and family members who uplift and inspire you, and avoid those who bring you down or undermine your self-esteem.

It is also important to practice self-care and self-compassion. When you take care of yourself physically, mentally, and emotionally, you are better equipped to handle the challenges and stressors of life. Make time for activities that nourish your body and soul, such as exercise, meditation, hobbies, and spending time in nature. And when you make mistakes or experience setbacks, be kind and forgiving to yourself. Remember that failure is a natural part of the learning and growth process, and that every mistake is an opportunity to learn and improve.

Confidence is not about being perfect or having all the answers. It is about being authentic, vulnerable, and true to yourself. When you embrace your imperfections and own your story, you become more relatable and approachable to others. You also become more resilient and adaptable, able to bounce back from setbacks and challenges with grace and determination.

Ultimately, confidence is about living fearlessly and embracing your full potential. It is about taking risks, pursuing your passions, and making a positive impact on the world around you. When you have confidence, you have the courage to stand up for what you believe in, even in the face of opposition or adversity. You have the strength to persevere through tough times, and the resilience to bounce back from setbacks and failures.

For men, women, teenagers, and children alike, confidence is a valuable asset that can help us navigate through life's ups and downs with grace and resilience.

It is the key to building strong relationships, achieving our goals, and living a fulfilling and purposeful life.

So how can we cultivate confidence in our daily lives? Here are some practical tips and exercises to get you started:

1. Practice positive self-talk: Pay attention to your inner dialogue and replace negative self-talk with positive affirmations. Remind yourself of your strengths, accomplishments, and unique qualities.

2. Set realistic goals: Break down your big goals into smaller, manageable steps and celebrate each milestone along the way. Focus on progress, not perfection.

3. Take risks: Step out of your comfort zone and try new things. Embrace failure as a learning opportunity and use it to build resilience and determination.

4. Practice self-care: Take care of your physical, mental, and emotional health through exercise, healthy eating, rest, and stress-management techniques.

5. Surround yourself with positive people: Seek out mentors, friends, and family members who support and encourage you. Avoid toxic relationships that undermine your self-esteem.

6. Embrace your authentic self: Be true to yourself and your values. Don't try to be someone you're not or live up to others' expectations.

7. Practice gratitude: Focus on the positive aspects of your life and express gratitude for the blessings and opportunities you have.

By incorporating these practices into your daily life, you can cultivate a sense of self-belief, self-confidence, and self-esteem. You can become the confident, empowered individual you were meant to be, ready to take on the world with courage and determination.

Remember, confidence is not about being perfect or having all the answers. It is about being authentic, vulnerable, and true to yourself. It is about embracing your strengths and weaknesses and trusting in your own judgment and abilities.

So, embrace your true self, embrace your confidence, and live fearlessly. The world is waiting for you to make your mark, and with confidence by your side, there is nothing you cannot achieve.

Where does it come from?

Confidence Where does it come from? How to Cultivate Confidence in Every Aspect of Your Life," we delve into the sources of confidence and how it can be nurtured in people of all ages and backgrounds. Confidence is a skill that can be cultivated and refined over time, rather than being an inherent or unchangeable trait.

Confidence often arises from a blend of factors, including upbringing, experiences, and mindset.

Children who are encouraged to explore new experiences and learn from their setbacks are more likely to become confident adults. Likewise, teenagers who receive support in their pursuits and are equipped with the tools to face challenges are more prone to developing self-assurance.

As adults, we possess the ability to mold our own confidence through introspection, practice, and positive reinforcement. Setting objectives, taking chances, and learning from our failures can help us establish a robust foundation of self-assurance that will guide us through life's highs and lows.

Confidence is a crucial part for success in all aspects of life, regardless of age or gender. It is essential for reaching our maximum potential, whether in education, career, relationships, or personal development.

So, where does confidence originate? It comes from within – from a belief in oneself and a readiness to confront challenges head-on. By recognizing the sources of confidence and actively striving to nurture it, we can all become fearless in the pursuit of our aspirations and ambitions.

Confidence is not about being perfect or having all the answers. It is about being authentic, vulnerable, and true to yourself. When you embrace your imperfections and own your story, you become more relatable and approachable to others. You also become more resilient and adaptable, able to bounce back from setbacks and challenges with grace and determination.

Being confident is about living fearlessly and embracing your full potential. It is about taking risks, pursuing your passions, and making a positive impact on the world around you. When you have confidence, you have the courage to stand up for what you believe in, even in the face of opposition or adversity. You have the strength to persevere through tough times, and the resilience to bounce back from setbacks and failures.

By understanding the origins of confidence and actively working to cultivate it, we can all become fearless in our pursuit of our goals and dreams. Embrace your true self, embrace your confidence, and live fearlessly. The world is waiting for you to make your mark, and with confidence by your side, there is nothing you cannot achieve.

Are we born with confidence, or do we learn it?

The question of whether we are born with confidence or learn it has perplexed many individuals who look to cultivate and develop this essential trait. Confidence is a multifaceted characteristic that can be shaped by several factors, such as genetics, upbringing, and life experiences. While some individuals may have a naturally higher level of confidence, it is also a skill that can be acquired and refined over time.

Confidence plays a vital role in every aspect of life, regardless of age or gender. It can significantly affect relationships, academic performance, career success, and personal endeavors. Recognizing that confidence is not solely an inherent quality but also a skill that can be developed empowers individuals to take proactive steps to build their self-assurance and belief in themselves.

One effective way to cultivate confidence is through practice and repetition. By consistently stepping out of one's comfort zone and confronting challenges, individuals can gradually build their confidence and self-esteem. This process of facing fears and overcoming obstacles helps to reinforce the belief in one's abilities and strengthens the foundation of self-assurance.

The influence of one's environment and social interactions cannot be overlooked when it comes to developing confidence. Surrounding oneself with supportive and empowering individuals who provide encouragement and positive feedback can have a profound impact on one's confidence levels. Engaging in activities or hobbies that allow for personal growth and achievement can also contribute to a stronger sense of self-worth and confidence.

Moreover, practicing self-care and engaging in positive self-talk are powerful tools for boosting confidence and fostering a more positive self-image. By identifying and challenging negative beliefs or self-doubt, individuals can replace them with empowering thoughts and affirmations. This shift in mindset can lead to a more confident and self-assured approach to life, enabling individuals to tackle challenges with greater ease and resilience.

It is important to recognize that building confidence is an ongoing process that requires patience and persistence. Setbacks and failures are inevitable, but they should be viewed as opportunities for growth and learning rather than reasons to lose confidence. By embracing a growth mindset and focusing on progress rather than perfection, individuals can continue to develop and strengthen their confidence over time.

Furthermore, confidence is not about being perfect or having all the answers. It is about being authentic, vulnerable, and true to oneself. Embracing one's imperfections and unique qualities can lead to a more genuine and relatable presence, which can, in turn, inspire confidence in others. By owning one's story and being comfortable with vulnerability, individuals can cultivate a deeper sense of self-acceptance and confidence.

Whether confidence is innate or learned, the key takeaway is that it is a skill that can be developed and nurtured throughout one's life. By taking proactive steps to build confidence and self-assurance, individuals of all ages and backgrounds can unlock their full potential and thrive in every aspect of their lives. Through practice, positive social interactions, self-care, and a growth mindset, anyone can cultivate the confidence necessary to face life's challenges with resilience and determination.

The Role of Fear in Our Lives

Fear is a complex and powerful emotion that plays a significant role in shaping our lives. In the subchapter "The Role of Fear in Our Lives" from the book "Confidence: How to Cultivate Confidence in Every Aspect of Your Life," we explore the profound impact that fear can have on our decisions, behaviors, and overall perspective on life.

Fear is a universal experience that affects individuals of all ages and backgrounds. Whether it's the fear of failure, rejection, or the unknown, these fears can act as barriers, preventing us from reaching our full potential and living life to the fullest. For men, women, teenagers, and children alike, fear can be a common obstacle that hinders personal growth, limits opportunities, and stifles confidence.

To cultivate confidence in every aspect of our lives, it is crucial to understand the role that fear plays and develop strategies to overcome it. Fear can serve as a natural warning system, alerting us to potential dangers and helping us navigate challenging situations. However, when fear becomes overwhelming and debilitating, it can have a detrimental effect on our well-being and success.

One of the key steps in managing fear is recognizing its presence and acknowledging its impact on our lives. By bringing awareness to our fears, we can begin to understand their origins and develop a more objective perspective. This self-awareness allows us to challenge negative beliefs and thought patterns that contribute to our fears and replace them with more positive and empowering ones.

"Fearless" explores a range of practical strategies for managing fear and building confidence in the face of adversity. Mindfulness techniques, such as deep breathing and meditation, can help us stay grounded in the present moment and reduce the intensity of fear-based thoughts. Positive self-talk and affirmations can also be powerful tools for reshaping our internal dialogue and bolstering our self-belief.

Gradual exposure to fearful situations is another effective approach for overcoming fear. By confronting our fears in a controlled and incremental manner, we can desensitize ourselves to the perceived threat and build resilience. This process involves stepping outside of our comfort zones, taking calculated risks, and embracing uncertainty. As we face our fears head-on and experience success, our confidence grows, and we become more equipped to handle future challenges.

It is important to recognize that overcoming fear is a journey, and setbacks are a natural part of the process. Rather than becoming discouraged by temporary failures or obstacles, we can choose to view them as opportunities for learning and growth. By cultivating a growth mindset and focusing on progress rather than perfection, we can maintain a sense of momentum and motivation in the face of fear.

In addition to personal strategies, seeking support from others can be invaluable in managing fear and building confidence. Surrounding ourselves with positive and encouraging individuals who believe in our abilities and provide guidance can help us navigate challenging situations with greater ease. Sharing our fears and vulnerabilities with trusted friends, family members, or professionals can also provide a sense of relief and perspective.

Ultimately, by acknowledging the role of fear in our lives and actively working to overcome it, we can cultivate a sense of confidence, courage, and empowerment that permeates every aspect of our existence. Whether we are men, women, teenagers, or children, facing our fears and embracing uncertainty can open up a world of possibilities and allow us to live life to the fullest.

The Importance of Confidence in Achieving Success

Confidence is a vital attribute that plays a significant role in deciding one's success in various aspects of life. It is a quality that transcends age and gender, and its importance cannot be overstated. Whether you are a man, woman, teenager, or child, possessing a powerful sense of self-assurance can be the key to unlocking your full potential and achieving your goals.

Confidence is the foundation upon which success is built. It provides individuals with the courage to take risks, step outside their comfort zones, and seize opportunities that come their way. When faced with challenges or obstacles, confidence acts as a driving force, enabling individuals to persevere and overcome difficulties. It allows them to believe in their abilities, trust their instincts, and make decisions with conviction.

For men, confidence can be a meaningful change in their personal and professional lives. It can help them excel in their careers, take on leadership roles, and build strong, meaningful relationships. Confident men are more likely to assert themselves, communicate effectively, and inspire others to follow their lead. They are not afraid to take calculated risks and are resilient in the face of setbacks.

Similarly, for women, confidence is a powerful tool that can help them break through gender barriers and shatter glass ceilings. It empowers them to speak up for themselves, advocate for their rights, and pursue their ambitions fearlessly. Confident women are more likely to embrace their unique strengths, challenge societal norms, and inspire other women to do the same.

For teenagers and children, developing confidence at an early age can set the stage for a lifetime of success and self-belief. It can help them navigate the challenges of growing up, build healthy relationships, and pursue their passions with enthusiasm. Confident teenagers are more likely to resist peer pressure, stand up for their beliefs, and make positive choices that align with their values.

Cultivating confidence is a lifelong journey that requires introspection, self-awareness, and a willingness to challenge limiting beliefs. It involves developing a positive mindset, setting achievable goals, and surrounding oneself with supportive individuals who believe in and encourage personal growth.

One effective way to boost confidence is to focus on personal strengths and accomplishments. Recognizing and celebrating one's successes, no matter how small, can help build self-esteem and reinforce a positive self-image. It is also important to learn from failures and setbacks, viewing them as opportunities for growth and learning rather than as definitive roadblocks.

Another key aspect of building confidence is to challenge negative self-talk and replace it with positive affirmations. The way we speak to ourselves has a profound impact on our self-perception and belief in our abilities. By consciously reframing negative thoughts and focusing on positive self-talk, individuals can gradually reshape their mindset and boost their confidence.

In the book "Confidence: How to Cultivate Confidence in Every Aspect of Your Life," readers will find a wealth of practical strategies, mindset shifts, and empowering techniques to help them build unshakable confidence. Whether struggling with self-doubt, fear of failure, or imposter syndrome, this book serves as a comprehensive guide to overcoming personal barriers and unleashing one's true potential.

It is important to remember that confidence is not about being perfect or immune to mistakes. Rather, it is about embracing one's flaws, acknowledging strengths, and maintaining belief in oneself regardless of the challenges that arise. Confidence is the unwavering faith in one's ability to navigate life's ups and downs, learn from experiences, and continuously grow as an individual.

Confidence is a powerful catalyst for success in every aspect of life. It is a quality that knows no age or gender boundaries and has the potential to transform lives. By cultivating confidence through personal growth, positive self-talk, and a willingness to embrace challenges, individuals can unlock their true potential and achieve their dreams. With confidence as a guiding light, there are no limits to what one can accomplish.

How Fear Can Hold Us Back

Fear is a pervasive emotion that can permeate every aspect of our lives, holding us back from reaching our full potential and living the life we truly desire. Its insidious nature can manifest in many ways, causing us to doubt ourselves, hesitate in the face of opportunities, and remain trapped within the confines of our comfort zones. In my book, "Confidence: How to Cultivate Confidence in Every Aspect of Your Life," I delve into the myriad ways in which fear can hinder our progress and provide actionable strategies for overcoming its paralyzing grip.

One of the most significant ways fear can hold us back is by eroding our self-confidence. When we are consumed by fear, we may find ourselves questioning our abilities, doubting our decisions, and hesitating to take decisive action. This self-doubt can be a formidable obstacle, preventing us from seizing opportunities and pursuing our goals with the unwavering determination necessary for success. By recognizing the insidious nature of fear and learning to cultivate a deep trust in ourselves, we can begin to break free from this self-limiting mindset and embrace our true potential.

Another way fear can hold us back is by keeping us firmly entrenched within the familiar confines of our comfort zones. The prospect of venturing into uncharted territory, whether it be in our personal or professional lives, can be daunting, causing us to shy away from new experiences and growth opportunities. However, it is often in these moments of discomfort and uncertainty that the most profound growth and fulfillment can be found. By pushing past our fear and embracing the unknown, we open ourselves up to a world of possibilities and the chance to discover new facets of ourselves.

In this book, I provide readers with a comprehensive toolkit of practical tips and exercises designed to help them build unshakable confidence and overcome the debilitating effects of fear. By cultivating a robust sense of self-belief, learning to embrace discomfort as a catalyst for growth, and taking incremental steps towards our goals, we can gradually break free from the grip of fear and live more boldly and authentically.

The journey of navigating and overcoming fear is one that is relevant to individuals of all ages and occupations. Whether you are a man, woman, teenager, or child, developing the skills and mindset necessary to confront and conquer fear is essential for building confidence in every aspect of your life. By understanding the ways in which fear can hold us back and actively working to challenge and overcome it, we can tap into our innate potential and live with the courage and resilience necessary to thrive in the face of life's challenges.

It is important to recognize that overcoming fear is not a one-time event, but rather an ongoing process that requires consistent effort and dedication. It involves developing a keen awareness of our thought patterns and emotional responses and learning to reframe negative self-talk into empowering affirmations. It also requires a willingness to step outside of our comfort zones, embrace vulnerability, and view failures as opportunities for growth and learning.

The path to living fearlessly is one of self-discovery and personal transformation. It is a journey that requires us to confront our deepest fears, challenge our limiting beliefs, and cultivate a deep sense of self-compassion and acceptance. By doing so, we can begin to live with greater authenticity, purpose, and joy, unburdened by the constraints of fear and self-doubt.

Fear is a powerful force that can hold us back from living the life we truly desire. By understanding its impact and actively working to overcome it, we can build the confidence necessary to pursue our dreams, take bold risks, and live with courage and resilience. Through the strategies and insights provided in "Fearless," readers will gain the tools and mindset necessary to break free from the grip of fear and unlock their full potential in every aspect of their lives.

Chapter 2: Overcoming Fear

Identifying Your Fears:

Fear is an inherent part of the human experience, a primal emotion that has helped our species survive for millennia. However, when left unchecked, fear can become a debilitating force that holds us back from reaching our full potential and living the life we truly desire. To cultivate genuine confidence in every aspect of our lives, it is crucial that we first find and understand the fears that exist within us.

This process of self-reflection and introspection is relevant to all individuals, regardless of age or gender. Men, women, teenagers, and children alike can receive help from taking the time to recognize and acknowledge the fears that shape their thoughts, emotions, and behaviors. By shining a light on these often-hidden parts of ourselves, we can begin to address them head-on and work towards overcoming their limiting influence.

To start this journey of self-discovery, set aside some quiet time to reflect on the things that make you feel anxious, uneasy, or insecure. These fears may manifest in various areas of your life, such as relationships, career, personal growth, or social interactions. Ask yourself questions like: Are you afraid of failure, rejection, or judgment from others? Do you have a fear of the unknown, of taking risks, or of stepping outside your comfort zone? By pinpointing these specific fears, you can begin to unravel their root causes and gain a deeper understanding of how they are changing your confidence and holding you back from living your best life.

It's important to remember that everyone experiences fear, and there is no shame in admitting to and confronting these emotions. In fact, it is a sign of strength and courage to acknowledge your fears and take proactive steps towards overcoming them. Once you have identified your fears, the next step is to challenge them. Question the validity of these fears and whether they are based in reality or simply products of your imagination. Often, our fears are exaggerated or unfounded, fueled by past experiences, societal pressures, or self-limiting beliefs. By confronting these fears with a rational and objective mindset, we can begin to see them for what they truly are – barriers to our growth and potential that can be overcome with the right tools and mindset.

Finding your fears is the first step towards cultivating confidence in every aspect of your life. It is a process that requires honesty, vulnerability, and a willingness to confront the parts of yourself that may feel uncomfortable or scary. But by doing so, you are taking a bold and necessary step towards reclaiming your power and creating the life you truly desire. Remember, it is okay to be afraid, but it is not okay to let those fears dictate your life. Embrace your fears, confront them with courage and determination, and watch as your confidence grows stronger with each passing day.

Strategies for Confronting and Overcoming Fear:

Fear is an inevitable part of the human experience, a natural response to perceived threats or challenges. While fear plays a crucial role in keeping us safe from danger, it can also become a debilitating force that holds us back from reaching our full potential and living the life we truly desire. To cultivate confidence in every aspect of our lives, it is essential that we develop effective strategies for confronting and overcoming fear.

One of the most powerful strategies for confronting fear is to face it head-on. It's natural to want to avoid the things that scare us, but doing so only gives our fears more power over us. By choosing to confront our fears directly, we take back control and begin to chip away at their hold on our lives. This doesn't mean that we have to tackle our biggest fears all at once, but rather that we can challenge ourselves to confront them in small, manageable steps. By gradually exposing ourselves to the things that scare us, we can build up our confidence and resilience, proving to ourselves that we are capable of handling discomfort and uncertainty.

Another effective strategy for overcoming fear is to reframe the way we think about it. Instead of viewing fear as a signal to run away or avoid, we can choose to see it as an opportunity for growth and self-discovery.

By reframing our fears in a positive light, we can transform them from obstacles into powerful motivators for change. For example, if you have a fear of public speaking, instead of focusing on the potential for embarrassment or failure, you can choose to view it as an opportunity to share your ideas with others and make a positive impact. By shifting our perspective in this way, we can begin to approach our fears with curiosity and enthusiasm, rather than dread and avoidance.

In addition to facing our fears head-on and reframing our thoughts, practicing self-care is another crucial part of overcoming fear. When we are feeling scared or anxious, it's easy to neglect our physical and emotional needs, but doing so only makes it harder to cope with the challenges we face. By prioritizing self-care, we give ourselves the resources and resilience we need to confront our fears with strength and clarity. This could include things like getting enough sleep, eating well, exercising regularly, and engaging in activities that bring us joy and relaxation. By taking care of ourselves in this way, we create a foundation from which to tackle our fears and cultivate confidence in every aspect of our lives.

Finally, it's important to remember that overcoming fear is a process, not a one-time event. It's okay to feel afraid, and it's normal to have setbacks and moments of doubt along the way. The key is to keep pushing forward, even when it feels hard or uncomfortable. By consistently confronting our fears and pushing ourselves outside of our comfort zones, we can cultivate the confidence and resilience we need to live our best lives. This is a journey that requires patience, persistence, and self-compassion, but the rewards are more than worth it.

Fear is a natural part of being human, but it doesn't have to control us. By using these strategies for confronting and overcoming fear – facing it head-on, reframing our thoughts, practicing self-care, and embracing the journey – we can cultivate the confidence we need to thrive in every aspect of our lives. Remember, you are stronger than you think, and with the right tools and mindset, you can overcome any fear that stands in your way.

Building Resilience in the Face of Fear

In the face of fear, cultivating resilience is essential to developing confidence in every aspect of your life. Fear has the power to paralyze us, to hold us back from pursuing our dreams and reaching our full potential. But by building resilience, we can learn to face our fears head-on, to weather the storms of life with courage and determination, and to appear stronger and more confident on the other side.

One of the key ways to build resilience in the face of fear is through the practice of self-care. When we are feeling scared or overwhelmed, it's easy to neglect our own needs and well-being, but doing so only makes it harder to cope with the challenges we face. By prioritizing self-care, we give ourselves the physical, emotional, and mental resources we need to navigate difficult situations with strength and clarity. This could include things like getting enough sleep, eating a healthy diet, exercising regularly, and engaging in activities that bring us joy and relaxation. By taking care of ourselves in this way, we create a solid foundation from which to confront our fears and build the resilience we need to thrive.

Another important aspect of building resilience is developing a growth mindset. Too often, we view failure or setbacks as evidence of our own inadequacy, as proof that we are not good enough or capable enough to achieve our goals. But by shifting our perspective and embracing a growth mindset, we can learn to see these challenges as opportunities for learning and growth. Instead of beating ourselves up for our mistakes or shortcomings, we can choose to approach them with curiosity and self-compassion, asking ourselves what we can learn from the experience and how we can use it to become stronger and more resilient in the future. By reframing failure in this way, we can cultivate the mental toughness and adaptability we need to bounce back from setbacks and keep moving forward with confidence.

In addition to practicing self-care and developing a growth mindset, surrounding ourselves with a supportive community is another key component of building resilience. When we are facing our fears or navigating difficult situations, it can be easy to feel alone and isolated, like we are the only ones struggling or facing challenges. But by reaching out to others and building a network of supportive friends, family, or mentors, we can tap into a powerful source of strength and encouragement. These people can provide us with the emotional support and guidance we need to navigate challenging situations with confidence, reminding us of our own inherent worth and potential, and helping us to see the bigger picture when we are feeling lost or overwhelmed.

Building resilience in the face of fear is a journey that requires patience, practice, and self-reflection. It's not about becoming fearless or invulnerable, but rather about developing the tools and mindset we need to face our fears with courage and grace, to learn from our experiences, and to keep moving forward with confidence and purpose. This is a process that looks different for everyone, and there is no one-size-fits-all approach to cultivating resilience. But by taking small steps every day to prioritize self-care, embrace a growth mindset, and surround ourselves with supportive people, we can gradually build the resilience we need to overcome any obstacle that comes our way.

Fear is a natural and inevitable part of life, but it doesn't have to hold us back from living the life we truly desire. By cultivating resilience in the face of fear, we can learn to face our challenges with courage and confidence, to bounce back from setbacks and failures, and to emerge stronger and more capable on the other side. Remember, you are more resilient than you think, and with the right tools and mindset, you can conquer your fears and thrive in every aspect of your life.

Chapter 3: Cultivating Confidence

Recognizing Your Strengths and Abilities

Recognizing your strengths and abilities is a fundamental step in building confidence in all areas of your life. Self-doubt and insecurities can be major obstacles to reaching your full potential, but by taking the time to identify and embrace your unique talents and skills, you can boost your self-esteem and develop self-assurance.

Everyone, regardless of age or gender, has their own set of strengths and abilities. It's crucial to understand that each person is unique, and what comes naturally to one individual may be a struggle for another. By focusing on your own specific strengths, you can begin to appreciate your value and worth.

One effective way to show your strengths is to reflect on past experiences and accomplishments. Consider moments when you excelled or felt particularly confident in a certain activity or task. These instances can offer valuable insights into your natural talents and abilities. For example, if you find that public speaking came easily to you during a school presentation, this may show a strength in communication and self-expression.

Another helpful exercise is to seek feedback from others. Friends, family members, teachers, or colleagues can offer a fresh perspective on your strengths and abilities, highlighting qualities that you may not have recognized in yourself. They may notice how you always are calm under pressure, or how you have a knack for creative problem-solving. By gathering input from others, you can gain a more well-rounded understanding of your strengths.

Once you have identified your strengths and abilities, it's important to nurture and develop them. This may involve setting specific goals related to your strengths, seeking out opportunities for growth and learning, or surrounding yourself with supportive individuals who can help you cultivate your talents. For instance, if you discover a strength in leadership, you might volunteer to lead a project at work or in your community to further develop this skill.

It's also important to acknowledge that everyone has areas where they can improve. Recognizing your weaknesses is not a sign of failure, but rather an opportunity for growth. By naming areas where you struggle, you can take steps to build your skills and knowledge, further boosting your confidence.

Remember, recognizing your strengths and abilities is not about comparing yourself to others or seeking perfection. It's about understanding and appreciating your unique qualities and using them to your advantage. By embracing your strengths, you can build a solid foundation of confidence that will empower you to tackle challenges, pursue your goals, and live a fulfilling life.

In summary, recognizing your strengths and abilities is a crucial step in cultivating confidence. Take time to reflect on your past successes, seek feedback from others, and actively work to develop your talents. By understanding and embracing your unique qualities, you can build a personal sense of self-assurance that will serve you well in all aspects of your life.

Setting Realistic Goals for Yourself

Setting realistic goals is a key component of building confidence in every aspect of your life. Whether you are a man, woman, teenager, or child, having clear and achievable goals can provide direction, motivation, and a sense of accomplishment that will boost your self-assurance.

When setting goals, it's important to start by understanding your strengths and weaknesses. Take an honest look at what you excel at and what areas you need to improve upon. This self-awareness will help you set goals that are challenging yet attainable, allowing you to build confidence as you make progress.

It's also crucial to set specific and measurable goals. Rather than making vague statements like "I want to be more confident," try setting concrete objectives such as "I will volunteer to lead one project at work this quarter" or "I will engage in one new social activity each month." Specific goals provide a clear target to work towards and make it easier to track your progress.

When setting goals, it's important to strike a balance between ambition and realism. While it's great to dream big, setting goals that are too far out of reach can be discouraging and may undermine your confidence if you do not achieve them. On the other hand, setting goals that are too easy won't provide the sense of achievement that comes from pushing yourself outside your comfort zone.

One effective strategy is to break larger goals down into smaller, manageable steps. For example, if your goal is to run a marathon, you might start by setting smaller goals like running a 5K or 10K race. By achieving these smaller milestones, you can build momentum and confidence as you work towards your ultimate goal.

Another key aspect of setting realistic goals is being flexible and adaptable. Life is unpredictable, and there will be times when your circumstances or priorities change. When this happens, it's important to be willing to adjust your goals accordingly. Don't view this as a failure, but rather as a sign of resilience and adaptability.

It's also important to celebrate your successes along the way. Acknowledging your achievements, no matter how small, can provide a powerful boost to your confidence and motivation. Take time to reflect on your progress and give yourself credit for the challenging work you've put in.

Finally, remember that setbacks and failures are a normal part of the growth process. No one achieves their goals without meeting obstacles along the way. When you face a setback, try to view it as a learning opportunity rather than a failure. Ask yourself what you can learn from the experience and how you can use that knowledge to improve going forward.

Setting realistic goals is a powerful tool for building confidence in every aspect of your life. By understanding your strengths and weaknesses, setting specific and measurable aims, breaking larger goals into manageable steps, being adaptable, celebrating your successes, and learning from setbacks, you can cultivate a confidence and self-assurance that will serve you well in all your endeavors. Remember, you have the power to achieve anything you set your mind to – all it takes is belief in yourself and the determination to keep moving forward.

Practicing Self-Compassion and Positive Self-Talk

Cultivating confidence in every aspect of our lives is a journey that requires patience, persistence, and most importantly, self-compassion. One of the most effective ways to build self-assurance is by practicing self-compassion and engaging in positive self-talk.

Too often, we are our own harshest critics, holding ourselves to impossible standards and berating ourselves for even the smallest mistakes. This negative self-talk can be deeply damaging to our confidence and self-esteem, leading us to doubt our abilities and question our worth.

The first step in practicing self-compassion is to recognize that everyone, regardless of age or gender, is imperfect and makes mistakes. Instead of judging ourselves harshly, we can choose to treat ourselves with kindness, understanding, and forgiveness. This means acknowledging our flaws and failings without letting them define us, and extending the same compassion to ourselves that we would offer a close friend.

One powerful way to practice self-compassion is through mindfulness. By bringing our attention to the present moment and seeing our thoughts and emotions without judgment, we can cultivate a sense of acceptance and understanding. When we notice negative self-talk arising, we can acknowledge it without getting caught up in it, and gently redirect our thoughts to something more positive.

Another key aspect of self-compassion is learning to set realistic expectations for ourselves. Often, we hold ourselves to impossibly ambitious standards, setting ourselves up for disappointment and self-criticism when we inevitably fall short. By setting realistic goals and celebrating our progress along the way, we can build a sense of accomplishment and self-worth that is not contingent on perfection.

In addition to practicing self-compassion, engaging in positive self-talk is another powerful tool for building confidence. The way we talk to ourselves has a profound impact on our mood, motivation, and self-image. By consciously choosing to speak to ourselves with kindness, encouragement, and optimism, we can rewire our brains to focus on our strengths and potential rather than our perceived shortcomings.

One effective way to practice positive self-talk is through affirmations. Affirmations are short, positive statements that we repeat to ourselves to reinforce a desired belief or attitude. For example, instead of telling ourselves "I'm not good enough," we might repeat the affirmation "I am capable, worthy, and deserving of success." By regularly practicing affirmations, we can gradually shift our self-talk from negative to positive, boosting our confidence and resilience in the face of challenges.

It's important to note that practicing self-compassion and positive self-talk is not about denying or suppressing negative emotions. It's natural to feel frustrated, disappointed, or discouraged at times, and it's important to acknowledge and process these feelings in a healthy way. However, by treating ourselves with kindness and understanding, and focusing on our strengths and potential, we can cultivate a sense of resilience and self-assurance that allows us to bounce back from setbacks and keep moving forward.

Building confidence is an ongoing process that requires patience, practice, and self-reflection. By making self-compassion and positive self-talk a regular part of our daily routines, we can gradually chip away at the negative beliefs and self-doubts that hold us back and cultivate a deep sense of self-assurance that allows us to pursue our goals with confidence and resilience.

Practicing self-compassion and positive self-talk are essential tools for building confidence in every aspect of our lives. By treating ourselves with kindness, setting realistic expectations, and focusing on our strengths and potential, we can cultivate self-worth and resilience that will serve us well in all our endeavors. Remember, building confidence is a journey, not a destination – so be patient with yourself, celebrate your progress, and never give up on your ability to achieve remarkable things.

Chapter 4: Confidence in Different Areas of Your Life

Building Confidence in Your Career

Building confidence in your career is essential for achieving success and satisfaction in your professional life. Whether you are just starting out in your chosen field or looking to advance in your current position, cultivating a strong sense of self-assurance can make a significant difference in your ability to overcome challenges, seize opportunities, and reach your goals.

One of the most important steps in building confidence in your career is setting clear, achievable goals for yourself. By taking the time to define what you want to accomplish and creating a roadmap to get there, you can prove a sense of direction and purpose that will keep you motivated and focused, even in the face of obstacles or setbacks. Start by naming your long-term career aspirations, then break them down into smaller, more manageable milestones that you can work towards on a daily or weekly basis.

As you progress in your career, it's crucial to continuously improve your skills and knowledge to stay competitive and confident in your abilities. Take advantage of every opportunity for professional development, whether it's attending workshops and seminars, pursuing added certifications or degrees, or simply reading industry publications to stay up to date on the latest trends and best practices. By investing in your own growth and learning, you'll not only increase your value to your employer but also boost your self-confidence and sense of accomplishment.

Networking is another powerful tool for building confidence in your career. By connecting with colleagues, mentors, and industry leaders, you can gain valuable insights, advice, and support that can help you navigate challenges and seize new opportunities. Attend industry events, join professional organizations, and don't be afraid to reach out to people you admire for guidance or collaboration. Building a strong network of contacts can open doors to new possibilities and give you the confidence to pursue your goals with greater assurance.

Perhaps most importantly, building confidence in your career requires a strong belief in yourself and your abilities. Remember that everyone faces challenges and setbacks at some point in their professional journey, but it's how you respond to these obstacles that will ultimately determine your success. Instead of dwelling on your mistakes or limitations, focus on your strengths, accomplishments, and the progress you've made so far. Celebrate your victories, no matter how small, and use them as fuel to keep pushing forward.

When you do encounter setbacks or failures, try to view them as valuable learning experiences rather than personal shortcomings. Ask yourself what you can take away from each challenge and how you can use that knowledge to improve and grow in the future. By maintaining a growth mindset and staying committed to your own development, you'll be better equipped to handle whatever comes your way with confidence and resilience.

Building confidence in your career is an ongoing process that requires patience, perseverance, and a willingness to step outside your comfort zone. By setting clear goals, continuously improving your skills, networking with others, and believing in yourself, you can cultivate the self-assurance needed to thrive in every aspect of your professional life. Remember, confidence is not an innate trait but rather a muscle that can be strengthened and developed over time. So, start taking steps today to build your confidence and watch as new opportunities and successes unfold before you.

Nurturing Confidence in Your Relationships

Nurturing confidence in your relationships is a crucial component of building a strong, healthy, and fulfilling life. Whether you are a man, woman, teenager, or child, the quality of your relationships can have a profound impact on your overall well-being, happiness, and success. By cultivating confidence in your interactions with others, you can create deeper, more meaningful connections and foster a greater sense of belonging and self-assurance.

One of the most important aspects of nurturing confidence in your relationships is effective communication. Being able to express your thoughts, feelings, and needs clearly and respectfully is essential for building trust, understanding, and intimacy with others. This means not only speaking your truth but also actively listening to and validating the perspectives of those around you. By engaging in open, honest, and compassionate dialogue, you can create a safe and supportive space for all parties to be heard and understood.

Another key component of nurturing confidence in your relationships is setting and keeping healthy boundaries. Boundaries are the limits we set for ourselves and others to protect our time, energy, and emotional well-being. By clearly communicating your boundaries and respecting those of others, you show self-respect and set up a foundation of mutual trust and consideration. This can be especially important in close relationships, where it's easy to fall into patterns of over-giving or over-accommodating at the expense of your own needs and desires.

Cultivating empathy and understanding is also crucial for building confidence in your relationships. Being able to put yourself in someone else's shoes and see things from their perspective can help you navigate conflicts, misunderstandings, and differences with greater ease and compassion. By approaching your relationships with a spirit of curiosity, openness, and non-judgment, you can foster deeper levels of connection and understanding that will strengthen your bonds and boost your confidence in your ability to relate to others.

It's important to remember that nurturing confidence in your relationships is an ongoing process that requires patience, effort, and self-reflection. There will be times when you struggle to communicate effectively, set boundaries, or practice empathy, and that's okay. What matters is that you stay committed to your own growth and the health of your relationships, even in the face of challenges or setbacks.

One powerful way to support your confidence in relationships is to surround yourself with people who uplift, inspire, and encourage you to be your best self. Seek out friends, family members, and partners who share your values, respect your boundaries, and celebrate your successes. By building a strong network of positive, supportive relationships, you'll have a solid foundation of love and acceptance to fall back on when times get tough.

At the same time, don't be afraid to let go of relationships that no longer serve you or align with your goals and values. It's natural for people to grow and change over time, and sometimes that means parting ways with those who no longer fit into your life. By being honest with yourself and others about your needs and expectations, you can make space for new, more fulfilling connections to enter your life.

Nurturing confidence in your relationships is about investing in yourself and the people around you. By prioritizing effective communication, healthy boundaries, empathy, and self-reflection, you can build stronger, more resilient connections that will support you through all of life's difficulties. Remember, the quality of your relationships is a direct reflection of the love and respect you have for yourself, so start by cultivating confidence from within, and watch as your relationships flourish and thrive.

Developing Confidence in Your Personal Growth

Developing confidence in your personal growth is a fundamental aspect of living a fulfilling and fearless life. Regardless of your age or gender, having a keen sense of self-assurance and belief in your abilities is essential for achieving success and happiness in every side of your existence.

The first step in cultivating confidence in your personal growth is to gain a deep understanding of your strengths and weaknesses. Take the time to engage in honest self-reflection and identify the areas in which you excel and those that require improvement. This process of self-awareness is crucial, as it allows you to set realistic goals and create a roadmap for your personal development journey.

Once you have a clear picture of your starting point, it's time to challenge yourself and step outside of your comfort zone. Growth and confidence are often the results of pushing yourself to try new things and embrace new experiences. Whether it's learning a new language, taking up a musical instrument, or embarking on a solo travel adventure, stepping into unfamiliar territory can help you discover hidden talents and build resilience in the face of adversity.

As you navigate the path of personal growth, it's essential to surround yourself with a supportive network of individuals who believe in your potential and encourage your progress. Seek out mentors, friends, and family members who uplift and inspire you, and who are willing to provide guidance and constructive feedback along the way. Having a dedicated support system can help you stay motivated and accountable, even when faced with obstacles or setbacks.

Another key aspect of developing confidence in your personal growth is learning to celebrate your successes, no matter how small they may seem. Acknowledge your achievements and give yourself credit for the progress you've made, rather than focusing solely on the end goal. By recognizing and appreciating your own growth, you reinforce the belief in your abilities and cultivate a more positive self-image.

It's important to remember that personal growth is an ongoing journey, and setbacks are a natural part of the process. When faced with failure or disappointment, try to view these experiences as valuable lessons and opportunities for learning and improvement. Embrace a growth mindset, and approach challenges with curiosity and a willingness to adapt and evolve.

In addition to external factors, developing confidence in your personal growth also requires a commitment to self-care and inner work. Prioritize activities that nurture your physical, mental, and emotional well-being, such as regular exercise, mindfulness practices, and engaging in hobbies that bring you joy. By taking care of yourself and cultivating a positive relationship with your inner self, you create a strong foundation for confidence and resilience.

Developing confidence in your personal growth is a lifelong endeavor that requires dedication, patience, and a willingness to embrace change. By gaining self-awareness, stepping outside your comfort zone, surrounding yourself with support, celebrating your successes, learning from setbacks, and prioritizing self-care, you can cultivate a deep sense of self-assurance and fearlessly pursue your dreams. Remember, confidence is not a destination, but rather a journey of self-discovery and growth. Embrace the process, trust in your abilities, and watch as your confidence soars to new heights.

Confidence in Business

Confidence in business is a critical component of success, regardless of whether you're a seasoned entrepreneur, a young professional just starting out, or a student with aspirations of launching your own venture. Having faith in your abilities to achieve your goals, overcome obstacles, and navigate the complex world of business is essential for building strong relationships, making bold decisions, and taking calculated risks.

For individuals of all ages and genders, cultivating confidence in business begins with a deep belief in oneself and one's capabilities. It's crucial to recognize and embrace your unique strengths, skills, and qualities that differentiate you from others in your field. By focusing on your assets and taking pride in your accomplishments, you can project an air of confidence in every business interaction, from networking events to boardroom meetings.

Setting specific, achievable goals and working diligently towards them is a powerful way to build confidence in business. By setting up milestones and tracking your progress, you create a sense of accomplishment and forward momentum that reinforces your belief in your abilities. Celebrate each victory along the way, no matter how small, and use these successes as fuel to propel you towards even greater achievements.

Effective communication is another vital aspect of confidence in business. Whether you're pitching a groundbreaking idea to investors, negotiating a complex deal with a client, or leading a team through a challenging project, the ability to articulate your thoughts and ideas clearly and persuasively is essential. Developing effective communication skills, such as active listening, empathy, and assertiveness, can help you build rapport, influence others, and instill confidence in your abilities as a leader and collaborator.

It's important to recognize that confidence in business does not mean being infallible or immune to mistakes. In fact, true confidence is often characterized by a willingness to take risks, learn from failures, and continuously improve oneself and one's business practices. Embracing a growth mindset, in which challenges are viewed as opportunities for learning and development, can help you keep confidence even in the face of adversity.

Building a strong network of mentors, colleagues, and supporters is another key factor in developing confidence in business. Surrounding yourself with individuals who believe in your potential, offer guidance and constructive feedback, and celebrate your successes can provide a powerful source of motivation and encouragement. Seek out opportunities to connect with like-minded professionals, attend industry events, and engage in meaningful conversations that broaden your perspective and inspire innovative ideas.

In addition to external factors, confidence in business also stems from a commitment to personal and professional development. Continuously expanding your knowledge, skills, and ability through education, training, and hands-on experience can help you feel more self-assured and prepared to tackle new challenges. Staying up to date with industry trends, best practices, and emerging technologies can also give you a competitive edge and boost your confidence in your ability to adapt and thrive in an ever-changing business landscape.

Confidence in business is a multifaceted quality that requires ongoing cultivation and nurturing. By believing in yourself, setting and achieving goals, communicating effectively, embracing a growth mindset, building a supportive network, and investing in personal and professional development, you can develop the unshakeable confidence needed to succeed in any business endeavor. Remember, confidence is not about being perfect, but rather about having faith in your ability to learn, grow, and overcome any obstacle that stands in your way.

Confidence in your social life

Confidence in your social life is a crucial aspect of building meaningful connections, nurturing relationships, and thriving in various social situations. Regardless of your age or gender, having a strong sense of self-assurance in your interactions with others can significantly change your overall happiness, well-being, and success in life.

One of the most principal factors in developing confidence in your social life is learning to be comfortable and content with who you are as an individual. Embracing your unique qualities, accepting your strengths and weaknesses, and celebrating your authentic self can help you project an air of self-assurance that naturally attracts others to you. When you are genuinely comfortable in your own skin, you are less likely to be swayed by external validation or the opinions of others, allowing you to form more genuine and fulfilling connections.

Effective communication skills are another key part of building confidence in your social life. Being able to express yourself clearly, listen attentively, and engage in meaningful conversations can help you forge deeper, more meaningful relationships with others. Practice active listening by fully focusing on the person speaking, asking relevant questions, and showing empathy and understanding. By proving a genuine interest in others and their experiences, you can create an atmosphere of trust and openness that encourages authentic connections.

Setting healthy boundaries and asserting yourself when necessary is also essential for supporting confidence in your social interactions. Learning to say no to situations or people that do not align with your values or well-being is a powerful way to show self-respect and maintain an intense sense of self. When faced with disrespectful or manipulative behavior, it's important to stand up for yourself calmly and assertively, communicating your needs and expectations clearly. By proving and enforcing personal boundaries, you send a message that you value yourself and expect to be treated with respect, which can ultimately lead to more positive and fulfilling social experiences.

Cultivating a positive mindset is another crucial aspect of building confidence in your social life. Surrounding yourself with supportive, uplifting individuals who encourage your growth and celebrate your successes can help you keep a healthy perspective and boost your self-assurance. Engage in activities and hobbies that bring you joy and allow you to express your authentic self, as this can help you attract like-minded individuals who appreciate and value your unique qualities.

It's important to remember that building confidence in your social life is an ongoing process that requires practice, self-awareness, and a willingness to step outside your comfort zone. Embrace opportunities to engage in new social situations, even if they initially feel challenging or intimidating. By gradually exposing yourself to a variety of social experiences, you can develop resilience, adaptability, and a greater sense of self-assurance in navigating diverse social landscapes.

Additionally, practicing self-compassion and learning to be kind to yourself is essential for supporting confidence in your social life. Recognize that everyone makes mistakes, experiences awkward moments, and faces rejection at times. Instead of dwelling on negative experiences or engaging in self-criticism, focus on learning from these situations and using them as opportunities for personal growth and development.

Confidence in your social life is a reflection of your inner relationship with yourself. By cultivating self-acceptance, effective communication skills, healthy boundaries, a positive mindset, and a willingness to embrace new experiences, you can develop an unshakeable sense of self-assurance that allows you to navigate social situations with ease and grace. Remember, true confidence comes from within, and by nurturing a strong, positive relationship with yourself, you can create a foundation for building meaningful, fulfilling connections with others.

Confidence in school

Confidence in school is a vital part of a student's academic success and overall well-being. When students have a strong belief in their abilities and feel self-assured in their learning environment, they are more likely to actively take part in class discussions, ask questions when they need clarification, and approach challenges with a positive, growth-oriented mindset. This confidence not only enhances academic performance but also fosters the development of essential life skills such as resilience, perseverance, and adaptability.

Regardless of age or gender, cultivating confidence in school begins with recognizing and embracing one's unique strengths and talents. It's essential for students to understand that everyone has different aptitudes and learning styles, and that success is not defined by perfection, but rather by personal growth and progress. By focusing on their individual strengths and celebrating their accomplishments, students can develop a healthy sense of self-worth and confidence in their ability to overcome academic challenges.

Maintaining a positive self-image and engaging in regular self-care practices can also significantly contribute to a student's confidence in school. Encouraging students to prioritize their physical, mental, and emotional well-being by getting sufficient sleep, eating nutritious meals, staying physically active, and engaging in stress-reducing activities can help them feel more energized, focused, and self-assured in their academic pursuits. When students feel good about themselves and their overall health, they are more likely to approach their studies with enthusiasm and confidence.

Setting realistic, achievable goals and breaking them down into manageable steps is another effective strategy for building confidence in school. By setting up clear goals and creating a plan of action, students can feel more in control of their academic journey and experience a sense of accomplishment as they progress towards their goals. Celebrating milestones along the way, no matter how small, can provide a powerful boost to a student's confidence and motivation to continue striving for success.

Fostering positive relationships with teachers, classmates, and mentors is also crucial for nurturing confidence in school. When students feel supported, valued, and respected by those around them, they are more likely to take risks, express their ideas, and seek help when needed. Encouraging students to actively engage in classroom discussions, collaborate with their peers, and seek guidance from their teachers can help create a positive, inclusive learning environment that promotes confidence and personal growth.

In addition to external support, students can also develop confidence in school by cultivating a growth mindset. This involves viewing challenges and setbacks as opportunities for learning and improvement, rather than as failures or indications of personal inadequacy. By embracing the idea that intelligence and abilities can be developed through effort, persistence, and learning from mistakes, students can approach their academic pursuits with greater resilience and confidence in their potential for growth.

Encouraging students to explore their passions and engage in extracurricular activities can also play a significant role in building confidence in school. When students have the opportunity to pursue their interests and develop skills outside of the traditional classroom setting, they can discover new talents, build social connections, and experience a sense of accomplishment that carries over into their academic life. Participating in sports, clubs, volunteer work, or creative endeavors can help students develop a well-rounded sense of self and boost their overall confidence in their abilities.

Confidence in school is a multifaceted quality that requires ongoing nurturing and support from both the student and their educational community. By recognizing and celebrating individual strengths, prioritizing self-care, setting achievable goals, fostering positive relationships, embracing a growth mindset, and exploring personal interests, students can develop the self-assurance needed to thrive in their academic journey and beyond. Remember, confidence in school is not about perfection, but rather about believing in oneself, embracing challenges as opportunities for growth, and recognizing that every student has the potential to succeed and make a positive impact in the world.

Confidence in sports

Confidence in sports is a vital component of an athlete's success, regardless of their age, gender, or skill level. Whether you're a professional athlete competing on the world stage or a young child just starting to explore your love for a particular sport, having a powerful sense of self-belief and trust in your abilities can make a significant difference in your performance and overall enjoyment of the activity.

When an athlete has confidence in their skills and training, they are more likely to approach their sport with a positive, growth-oriented mindset. This confidence allows them to push past their perceived limits, embrace challenges as opportunities for improvement, and keep focus and composure in high-pressure situations. Confident athletes are also more likely to take calculated risks, experiment with new techniques, and learn from their mistakes, all of which contribute to their overall development and success in their chosen sport.

One of the most effective ways to cultivate confidence in sports is through consistent, purposeful practice and preparation. By dedicating time and effort to honing their skills, athletes can build a sturdy foundation of competence and self-assurance. This includes not only physical training but also mental preparation, such as setting achievable goals, visualizing success, and developing positive self-talk.

When athletes feel well-prepared and have a clear understanding of their strengths and areas for improvement, they are more likely to approach competition with a sense of confidence and readiness.

Another key aspect of building confidence in sports is learning to reframe setbacks and failures as valuable learning experiences. No athlete, regardless of their skill level, is immune to making mistakes or meeting obstacles. However, confident athletes view these challenges as opportunities for growth and development, rather than as indications of personal inadequacy. By embracing a growth mindset and focusing on the process of improvement rather than solely on outcomes, athletes can support a sense of confidence and resilience in the face of adversity.

Fostering a supportive, positive environment is also crucial for nurturing confidence in sports. When athletes feel encouraged, valued, and respected by their coaches, teammates, and loved ones, they are more likely to take risks, express their ideas, and persevere through grim times. Coaches can play a particularly key role in building confidence by providing constructive feedback, recognizing individual strengths, and creating a team culture that values effort, improvement, and collaboration.

It's important to note that confidence in sports is not about being perfect or always achieving victory. Instead, it's about having faith in one's abilities, trusting the process of growth and development, and supporting a positive, resilient attitude in the face of challenges. Confident athletes understand that setbacks and losses are a natural part of the journey, and they use these experiences as fuel for motivation and improvement.

In addition to the benefits for individual athletes, confidence in sports can also have a positive impact on team dynamics and performance. When a team is composed of confident, self-assured individuals who trust in their own abilities and those of their teammates, they are more likely to communicate effectively, work collaboratively, and support one another through both successes and failures. This collective confidence can lead to improved team cohesion, resilience, and overall success.

Cultivating confidence in sports is an ongoing process that requires dedication, self-awareness, and a willingness to embrace challenges as opportunities for growth. By consistently practicing and preparing, reframing setbacks as learning experiences, seeking support from others, and keeping a positive, growth-oriented mindset, athletes of all ages and skill levels can develop the self-assurance needed to thrive in their chosen sport. Remember, confidence in sports is not about being perfect, but rather about believing in oneself, embracing the journey of improvement, and recognizing that every athlete has the potential to achieve wonderful things when they trust in their own abilities.

Confidence in competition

Confidence in competition is a critical factor in achieving success, regardless of the field or level of competition. Whether you're a student taking part in an academic tournament, a business professional vying for a promotion, or an athlete striving for victory, having a keen sense of self-belief and trust in your abilities can significantly affect your performance and overall experience.

When individuals approach competition with confidence, they are more likely to keep focus, composure, and resilience in the face of challenges. Confident competitors are able to stay true to their own strengths and strategies, rather than being swayed by external pressures or the performance of others. They understand that success is not solely defined by winning or losing, but rather by the effort, growth, and learning that takes place throughout the competitive process.

One of the most effective ways to cultivate confidence in competition is through thorough preparation and practice. By dedicating time and energy to developing the necessary skills, knowledge, and strategies, individuals can build a strong foundation of competence and self-assurance. This preparation may involve studying relevant materials, rehearsing presentations or performances, or engaging in physical training and conditioning. When competitors feel well-prepared and have a clear understanding of their abilities and goals, they are more likely to approach the competitive situation with a sense of confidence and readiness.

Visualization and positive self-talk are also powerful tools for building confidence in competition. By mentally rehearsing successful outcomes and focusing on positive, affirming thoughts, individuals can create a mindset that is conducive to peak performance. This may involve visualizing oneself executing key skills flawlessly, overcoming obstacles, and achieving desired results. By regularly engaging in these mental practices, competitors can develop a strong sense of self-belief and trust in their abilities, even in the face of high-pressure situations.

Another key aspect of confidence in competition is learning to reframe setbacks and failures as valuable learning opportunities. No competitor, regardless of their skill level or experience, is immune to making mistakes or encountering challenges. However, confident competitors view these moments as chances to grow, adapt, and improve, rather than as indications of personal inadequacy. By embracing a growth mindset and focusing on the lessons learned from each experience, individuals can keep a sense of confidence and resilience, even in the face of adversity.

Seeking support and guidance from mentors, coaches, and peers can also play a significant role in fostering confidence in competition. When individuals feel encouraged, valued, and respected by those around them, they are more likely to take risks, express their ideas, and persevere through difficult times. Mentors and coaches can provide valuable feedback, guidance, and support, helping competitors to find their strengths, areas for improvement, and strategies for success. Similarly, surrounding oneself with positive, supportive peers can create a sense of camaraderie and shared purpose that bolsters confidence and motivation.

It's important to recognize that confidence in competition is not about being perfect or always achieving victory. Instead, it's about having faith in one's abilities, embracing the process of growth and development, and keeping a positive, resilient attitude in the face of challenges. Confident competitors understand that setbacks and losses are an integral part of the journey, and they use these experiences as fuel for motivation and improvement.

Ultimately, cultivating confidence in competition is an ongoing process that requires self-awareness, dedication, and a willingness to embrace challenges as opportunities for growth. By consistently preparing and practicing, using visualization and positive self-talk, reframing setbacks as learning experiences, seeking support from others, and supporting a growth-oriented mindset, individuals in any competitive field can develop the self-assurance needed to excel. Remember, confidence in competition is not about being flawless, but rather about believing in oneself, staying true to one's own strengths and strategies, and recognizing that every competitor has the potential to achieve remarkable things when they trust in their own abilities and embrace the journey of continuous improvement.

Chapter 5: Maintaining Confidence in the Face of Challenges

Dealing with Setbacks and Failures

Setbacks and failures are a natural part of life's journey, but how we respond to these challenges shapes our character and resilience. As you work towards cultivating confidence in every aspect of your life, it is crucial to develop the skills and mindset needed to bounce back from disappointments and overcome obstacles.

For individuals of all ages and backgrounds, encountering setbacks can be disheartening and discouraging. However, it is essential to recognize that failure is not a dead end, but rather a valuable opportunity for growth and learning. By embracing setbacks as stepping stones to success, you can build the resilience and confidence needed to navigate life's challenges with grace and determination.

One of the most effective strategies for dealing with setbacks is to practice self-compassion. Treat yourself with kindness and understanding, acknowledging that everyone makes mistakes and experiences disappointments. Instead of dwelling on the negative aspects of a setback, focus on the lessons you can learn from the experience and how they can contribute to your personal growth and development.

Maintaining a positive and optimistic mindset is another key factor in overcoming setbacks and failures. Rather than viewing these challenges as a reflection of your self-worth or capabilities, try to see them as temporary obstacles that can be overcome with perseverance and dedication. Surround yourself with supportive and encouraging individuals who can help you support a positive outlook and provide guidance and motivation during challenging times.

It is also important to remember that setbacks and failures do not define your potential or value as a person. Every successful individual has faced many challenges and disappointments on their path to achievement. By learning to navigate these obstacles with resilience and a growth mindset, you can cultivate the confidence needed to pursue your goals and aspirations fearlessly.

In times of setbacks and failures, practice self-reflection and analyze the situation objectively. Ask yourself what you can learn from the experience, what you might have done differently, and how you can apply these insights to future endeavors. By approaching setbacks as opportunities for self-improvement and skill development, you can transform disappointments into powerful catalysts for personal growth.

Dealing with setbacks and failures is an integral part of the journey towards cultivating confidence in every aspect of your life. By practicing self-compassion, keeping a positive mindset, and viewing challenges as opportunities for growth, you can develop the resilience and self-assurance needed to overcome any obstacle that comes your way. Embrace the lessons that setbacks offer and watch as your confidence grows stronger with each challenge you face.

Seeking Support and Guidance from Others

As you embark on the journey of cultivating confidence and becoming fearless in every aspect of your life, it is important to recognize the value of seeking support and guidance from others. Regardless of your age or background, having a network of trusted individuals who can offer advice, encouragement, and perspective can make a significant difference in your personal growth and self-assurance.

Surrounding yourself with positive and uplifting individuals is crucial for building and supporting confidence. Seek out mentors, friends, family members, or support groups who can provide guidance and support as you navigate the challenges and obstacles that arise on your path to fearlessness. These individuals can offer valuable insights, share their own experiences, and help you gain new perspectives on the situations you meet.

It is important to remember that asking for help is a sign of strength, not weakness. Recognizing when you need aid and having the courage to reach out to others shows self-awareness and a commitment to personal growth. By seeking guidance from those who have faced similar struggles or have ability in areas where you need support, you are taking proactive steps towards building your confidence and overcoming your fears.

In addition to providing guidance and advice, a supportive community can help you stay accountable, motivated, and focused on your goals. Sharing your fears, doubts, and insecurities with trusted individuals can help you gain clarity, receive encouragement, and feel less alone in your journey. By connecting with others who are also working towards cultivating confidence and fearlessness, you can create a sense of camaraderie and shared purpose that propels you forward.

When seeking support and guidance, it is essential to be open and receptive to feedback and constructive criticism. While it can be challenging to hear about areas where you need improvement, remember that this feedback is given with your best interests in mind. Embrace the opportunity to learn and grow from the perspectives and experiences of others and use their insights to develop new strategies for building confidence and overcoming obstacles.

Remember that seeking support and guidance is an ongoing process. As you continue your journey of personal growth and self-discovery, your needs and challenges may change. Be willing to adapt and seek out new sources of support and guidance, as necessary. By continuously expanding your network of positive influences and trusted advisors, you can create a sturdy foundation for lasting confidence and fearlessness.

Seeking support and guidance from others is a vital component of cultivating confidence in every aspect of your life. Embrace the wisdom, encouragement, and diverse perspectives that a supportive network can provide. By surrounding yourself with uplifting individuals, being open to feedback and guidance, and staying committed to your personal growth, you can create a powerful support system that empowers you to face challenges head-on and appear stronger, more confident, and truly fearless.

Embracing Change and Uncertainty

Change and uncertainty are inherent aspects of life, constantly reshaping our experiences and challenging us to adapt and grow. While many people fear the unknown and cling to the comfort of stability, embracing change and uncertainty is a powerful way to cultivate confidence in every aspect of your life. By learning to navigate new situations and challenges with grace and resilience, you can develop the flexibility and self-assurance needed to thrive in an ever-changing world.

One of the key strategies for embracing change and uncertainty is to focus on the present moment. Often, our fears and anxieties about the future can overwhelm us, causing us to feel paralyzed and unable to take action. By grounding yourself in the here and now, you can better assess your current situation, make informed decisions, and take proactive steps towards your goals. Practicing mindfulness and being fully engaged in the present can help you develop a sense of calm and clarity, even in the face of uncertainty.

Cultivating a mindset of curiosity and openness is another essential aspect of embracing change and uncertainty. Instead of viewing new experiences and challenges as threats, try to approach them with a sense of wonder and excitement. Recognize that each new situation presents an opportunity for learning, growth, and self-discovery. By keeping an open and adaptable mindset, you can more easily navigate the twists and turns of life, finding joy and meaning in the journey rather than fixating on the destination.

Embracing change and uncertainty also requires a willingness to step outside of your comfort zone. While it can be tempting to cling to the familiar and predictable, true growth and confidence often lie beyond the boundaries of what we know. By pushing yourself to try new things, take calculated risks, and face your fears head-on, you can expand your horizons and develop a greater sense of self-assurance. Remember that discomfort is often a sign that you are growing and evolving, and that each challenge you overcome strengthens your resilience and confidence.

Another key aspect of embracing change and uncertainty is to focus on the factors within your control. While you may not be able to predict or influence every outcome, you can always choose how you respond to and navigate the challenges that arise.

By focusing on your own attitudes, actions, and decisions, you can support a sense of agency and empowerment, even in the face of uncertainty. Trust in your ability to adapt, learn, and grow, and have faith that you own the strength and resourcefulness needed to overcome any obstacle.

It is also important to maintain a support system of trusted individuals who can offer guidance, encouragement, and perspective as you navigate change and uncertainty. Surround yourself with positive, adaptable, and resilient people who can inspire and motivate you to embrace new experiences and challenges. By sharing your fears, doubts, and successes with others, you can gain valuable insights, feel less alone, and build a sense of shared purpose and determination.

Embracing change and uncertainty is a lifelong practice that requires patience, self-awareness, and a commitment to personal growth. By staying present, cultivating curiosity and openness, stepping outside your comfort zone, focusing on what you can control, and leaning on a supportive network, you can develop the confidence and resilience needed to thrive in any situation. Remember that change and uncertainty are not obstacles to be feared, but opportunities to be embraced – opportunities to learn, grow, and discover the incredible strength and adaptability that lie within you. So, take a deep breath, trust in yourself, and step boldly into the unknown, knowing that each challenge you face is an invitation to become the most confident, fearless version of yourself.

Chapter 6: The Power of Fearlessness

Embracing Risk and Stepping Out of Your Comfort Zone

Cultivating true confidence in every aspect of your life requires embracing risk and stepping out of your comfort zone. This can be challenging, as fear and self-doubt often hold us back from reaching our full potential. However, pushing ourselves beyond our comfort zones leads to personal growth and the development of resilience, which is essential for facing any challenge that comes our way.

Stepping out of your comfort zone can lead to incredible opportunities for growth and self-discovery, regardless of age or gender. Trying a new hobby, taking on a leadership role, or pursuing a dream that seems out of reach are all examples of calculated risks that can lead to a more fulfilling and rewarding life. By embracing risk, you break free from the limitations imposed by fear and unlock your full potential.

To start embracing risk, set small, achievable goals that push you outside of your comfort zone. Taking on new challenges and experiencing small successes builds the confidence needed to tackle larger obstacles. Surrounding yourself with supportive and encouraging individuals can also help you take the necessary risks to grow and expand your horizons.

It's important to recognize that the path to true confidence is not always easy. It requires courage, determination, and a willingness to face the unknown. However, by consistently stepping out of your comfort zone and embracing risk, you develop the resilience and adaptability needed to navigate life's challenges with grace and confidence.

In addition to personal growth, embracing risk can also lead to significant professional and personal rewards. Taking calculated risks in your career, such as pursuing a new opportunity or proposing an innovative idea, can open doors to advancement and success. In your personal life, taking risks such as trying new experiences or forming new connections can enrich your relationships and broaden your perspectives.

It's essential to approach risk-taking with a growth mindset, viewing challenges as opportunities for learning and development rather than threats to be avoided. By reframing your perspective on risk and embracing the discomfort that comes with stepping outside of your comfort zone, you can cultivate a sense of fearlessness that permeates every aspect of your life.

Remember, the rewards of embracing risk often far outweigh the temporary discomfort or fear associated with taking that first step. By consistently challenging yourself to step outside of your comfort zone, you build the confidence and resilience needed to pursue your dreams and live a life of purpose and fulfillment.

So, don't let fear hold you back from unlocking your true potential. Embrace risk, step out of your comfort zone, and watch as your confidence soars to new heights. The power of fearlessness lies within you – all you need to do is take that first step.

Finding Courage to Pursue Your Dreams

Finding the courage to pursue your dreams can be challenging, especially when faced with fear and self-doubt. However, with the right mindset and strategies, you can overcome these obstacles and cultivate the confidence needed to turn your dreams into reality.

The first step in finding courage is to name your true passion and purpose. What drives you? What makes you feel fulfilled and alive? By understanding what truly motivates you, you can begin to take steps towards achieving your dreams with confidence and conviction. Take time to reflect on your values, strengths, and aspirations, and use this self-awareness to guide your actions and decisions.

Surrounding yourself with positive influences and support systems is crucial in finding the courage to pursue your dreams. Seek out friends, family members, mentors, or online communities who believe in you and your vision. Having a strong support network provides encouragement, guidance, and accountability as you navigate the challenges and uncertainties that come with chasing your dreams.

Reframing your mindset to embrace failure as a learning opportunity is another key aspect of finding courage. Failure is not a sign of weakness or inadequacy, but rather a stepping stone towards success. By viewing setbacks and challenges as opportunities for growth and improvement, you build the resilience and adaptability needed to push past your fears and pursue your dreams with confidence.

Practicing self-care and self-love is also essential in finding the courage to pursue your dreams. Taking care of your mental, emotional, and physical well-being provides you with the energy, clarity, and strength needed to face any obstacles that come your way. Engage in activities that bring you joy, prioritize rest and relaxation, and treat yourself with kindness and compassion.

Developing a plan of action and setting achievable goals can help you break down your dream pursuit into manageable steps. By creating a roadmap and celebrating small victories along the way, you build momentum and confidence in your ability to achieve your ultimate vision. Remember to be flexible and adaptable, as the path to your dreams may take unexpected turns and require adjustments along the way.

Another powerful strategy for finding courage is to surround yourself with inspiration and role models. Seek out stories of individuals who have overcome adversity and achieved their dreams and use their examples as motivation and guidance. Attend workshops, read books, or listen to podcasts that provide insights and strategies for cultivating courage and pursuing your passions.

Remember that finding courage is an ongoing practice that requires patience, self-compassion, and a willingness to step outside of your comfort zone. Embrace the discomfort and uncertainty that comes with pursuing your dreams, and trust in your ability to navigate challenges and appear stronger and more confident on the other side.

Finding the courage to pursue your dreams is a journey that requires self-awareness, supportive relationships, a growth mindset, self-care, actionable plans, inspiration, and a commitment to ongoing practice. By implementing these strategies and cultivating a fearless mindset, you can overcome fear and self-doubt and turn your dreams into a reality. Remember, you have the power within you to achieve anything you set your mind to – all you need is the courage to take that first step.

Inspiring Others to Cultivate Confidence in Their Lives

Confidence is a transformative trait that can positively change every aspect of an individual's life. As someone who has cultivated confidence in your own life, you have the power to inspire others to do the same, creating a ripple effect of positivity and empowerment.

One of the most effective ways to inspire confidence in others is to lead by example. Share your journey to confidence openly and authentically, highlighting both your successes and challenges along the way. By proving how you face your fears, take calculated risks, and push past your comfort zone, you serve as a powerful role model for others, showing them that confidence is attainable through practice and perseverance.

Encourage others to set meaningful goals for themselves and break them down into achievable steps. Offer support and guidance as they work towards their aims, celebrating their progress and helping them navigate setbacks and obstacles. By providing a safe and supportive environment for growth and self-discovery, you empower others to take ownership of their confidence development and pursue their dreams fearlessly.

Helping others recognize and appreciate their unique strengths and qualities is another key aspect of inspiring confidence. Encourage individuals to embrace their individuality and use their talents to their advantage. Provide genuine compliments and positive reinforcement, highlighting the ways in which their skills and perspectives contribute to their success and the success of those around them.

In addition to offering support and encouragement, it's essential to create opportunities for others to step outside of their comfort zones and build confidence through experience. Invite them to join you in trying new activities, taking on leadership roles, or pursuing challenging projects. By providing a safe and supportive environment for risk-taking and growth, you help others develop the resilience and adaptability needed to navigate life's challenges with confidence.

Another powerful way to inspire confidence in others is to foster a culture of continuous learning and development. Encourage individuals to seek out new knowledge and skills and provide resources and opportunities for personal and professional growth. By promoting a growth mindset and emphasizing the value of lifelong learning, you help others cultivate the confidence needed to embrace change, adapt to new situations, and pursue their full potential.

It's important to remember that inspiring confidence in others is an ongoing process that requires patience, empathy, and a genuine desire to uplift those around you. Be a consistent source of support and encouragement and be willing to have honest and compassionate conversations about the challenges and setbacks that inevitably arise on the path to confidence.

Recognize that inspiring confidence in others is not only a gift to them but also a powerful way to reinforce and strengthen your own confidence. By seeing the growth and transformation of those you inspire, you gain a deeper appreciation for the impact of your own journey and the importance of continuing to cultivate confidence in every aspect of your life.

Inspiring others to cultivate confidence in their lives is a noble and rewarding pursuit that has the power to transform individuals, communities, and the world at large. By leading by example, offering support and encouragement, creating opportunities for growth, fostering a culture of learning, and being a consistent source of inspiration, you can empower others to overcome their fears, pursue their dreams, and live a life of purpose and fulfillment. Remember, the ripple effect of confidence knows no bounds – by inspiring others, you create a world where everyone has the courage and self-assurance to reach their full potential.

What your life would look like if you had no confidence, doubt and fear

Imagine a life consumed by constant self-doubt, fear, and a lack of confidence. Every decision, no matter how small, becomes a source of anxiety and uncertainty. You second-guess your abilities, question your judgement, and hold yourself back from pursuing your passions and dreams.

In your personal life, a lack of confidence can lead to strained relationships and a sense of isolation. You may find it challenging to express your thoughts and feelings openly, fearing rejection or criticism from others. Social situations become sources of stress and discomfort, leading you to withdraw and miss valuable connections and experiences.

Your professional life may also suffer as a result of low confidence. You may struggle to assert yourself in meetings, express your ideas, or take on new responsibilities, hindering your career growth and advancement. The fear of failure or disapproval from colleagues and superiors can lead to a sense of stagnation and unfulfillment in your work.

Without confidence, it becomes difficult to set and achieve meaningful goals, as doubt and fear consistently undermine your efforts. You may find yourself settling for less than you deserve, both personally and professionally, as you lack the self-assurance needed to advocate for yourself and pursue your true desires.

A life without confidence can also take a toll on your mental and emotional well-being. Constant self-doubt and fear can lead to increased stress, anxiety, and even depression. You may find it challenging to keep a positive self-image or practice self-care, as you struggle to believe in your own worth and value.

The impact of low confidence can extend beyond your firsthand experiences, affecting your ability to make a positive difference in the world. You may hesitate to stand up for your beliefs, advocate for causes you care about, or create meaningful change, as fear and self-doubt hold you back from using your voice and talents for good.

However, it's important to recognize that a life without confidence, ruled by doubt and fear, is not an inevitable reality. By acknowledging the negative impact of low self-assurance and taking proactive steps to cultivate confidence, you can transform your life and unlock your full potential.

Through the practices and strategies outlined in "Confidence: How to Cultivate Confidence in Every Aspect of Your Life," you can learn to overcome self-doubt, conquer fear, and build the unshakeable confidence needed to pursue your dreams and live a life of purpose and fulfillment. By developing an intense sense of self, surrounding yourself with supportive individuals, embracing challenges as opportunities for growth, and practicing self-compassion, you can break free from the limitations of low confidence and create a life that truly reflects your values and aspirations.

Remember, confidence is not an innate trait, but rather a skill that can be developed and strengthened over time. By committing to the journey of self-discovery and personal growth, you can transform a life dominated by doubt and fear into one filled with courage, resilience, and the unwavering belief in your ability to achieve greatness. The power to create a confident, fulfilling life lies within you – all you need to do is take that first step.

Helping others get over their lack of confidence

Helping others overcome their lack of confidence is a powerful way to make a positive impact on their lives while simultaneously reinforcing and strengthening your own self-assurance. By offering support, guidance, and encouragement, you can empower individuals to break free from the limitations of self-doubt and fear and pursue their dreams with courage and conviction.

One of the most effective ways to help others build confidence is by actively listening to their concerns and experiences without judgment. Create a safe and supportive space where individuals feel comfortable sharing their thoughts, feelings, and challenges. By confirming their experiences and offering empathy and understanding, you help them feel heard, valued, and less alone in their struggles.

Another key strategy for boosting others' confidence is to help them find and celebrate their strengths and accomplishments. Encourage individuals to reflect on their unique talents, skills, and achievements, and provide specific, genuine praise and recognition for their efforts and successes. By highlighting their positive qualities and contributions, you help them develop a stronger sense of self-worth and belief in their abilities.

Sharing your own experiences and struggles with confidence can also be a powerful way to support others in their journey. By being open and honest about your own challenges and the strategies you've used to overcome them, you provide relatable examples and inspiration for others to draw upon. This vulnerability and authenticity can foster a sense of connection and trust, making others more receptive to your guidance and encouragement.

Encouraging others to set achievable goals and break them down into manageable steps is another effective way to help them build confidence. Help them in creating a plan of action and offer support and accountability as they work towards their objectives. Celebrate their progress and accomplishments along the way, no matter how small, to reinforce their sense of capability and maintain momentum.

In addition to offering support and encouragement, it's essential to provide others with opportunities to step outside their comfort zone and build confidence through experience. Invite them to join you in trying new activities, taking on leadership roles, or pursuing challenging projects. By creating a safe and supportive environment for risk-taking and growth, you help others develop the resilience and adaptability needed to navigate life's challenges with greater self-assurance.

Another powerful way to help others overcome their lack of confidence is to connect them with resources and tools for personal and professional development. Share books, articles, podcasts, or workshops that have been instrumental in your own confidence journey and encourage them to explore new avenues for learning and growth. By promoting a culture of continuous self-improvement and providing access to valuable resources, you empower others to take ownership of their confidence development and pursue their full potential.

Finally, it's important to remember that helping others build confidence is an ongoing process that requires patience, consistency, and a genuine desire to see others succeed. Be a reliable source of support and encouragement and celebrate their victories and milestones along the way. By investing in the growth and well-being of those around you, you not only contribute to their personal and professional success but also create a ripple effect of positivity and empowerment that extends far beyond your immediate circle.

Helping others overcome their lack of confidence is a noble and rewarding pursuit that has the power to transform lives and communities. By offering a listening ear, celebrating strengths and accomplishments, sharing your own experiences, encouraging goal setting, providing opportunities for growth, connecting others with resources, and being a consistent source of support, you can empower individuals to break free from the limitations of self-doubt and fear, and pursue a life of purpose and fulfillment. Remember, the impact of your efforts to boost others' confidence may extend far beyond what you can see – by uplifting those around you, you create a world where everyone has the courage and self-assurance to reach their full potential.

Chapter 7: The Real Difference Between Confidence and Cockiness

Confidence and cockiness are often mistaken for one another, but there is a crucial distinction between the two. Confidence is a positive and healthy trait that stems from a genuine belief in one's abilities, while cockiness is an exaggerated sense of self-importance that often masks underlying insecurities. Understanding the difference between these two qualities is essential for cultivating true self-assurance and building meaningful relationships with others.

Confidence is rooted in self-awareness, humility, and a realistic assessment of one's strengths and weaknesses. Confident individuals possess a quiet, inner strength that allows them to face challenges head-on, take calculated risks, and bounce back from setbacks. They understand that their worth is not defined by external validation or comparisons to others, but rather by their own personal growth and accomplishments.

Confident people are open to feedback and constructive criticism, recognizing that there is always room for improvement and learning. They are willing to admit when they are wrong or need help, and they approach others with empathy and respect. Confidence allows individuals to celebrate their successes without diminishing the achievements of others, and to uplift and inspire those around them.

In contrast, cockiness is characterized by an inflated ego, a sense of superiority, and a need to constantly prove oneself to others. Cocky individuals often boast about their accomplishments, belittle the efforts of others, and seek attention and admiration at any cost. They may appear self-assured on the surface, but their behavior often stems from deep-seated insecurities and a fear of vulnerability.

Cockiness can lead to a host of negative consequences, both personally and professionally. Cocky individuals may struggle to form genuine connections with others, as their arrogance and lack of empathy can be off-putting and alienating. They may also have difficulty accepting constructive feedback or admitting when they are wrong, hindering their personal and professional growth.

Moreover, cockiness can lead to risky or reckless behavior, as individuals may overestimate their abilities or underestimate potential challenges. This can result in poor decision-making, strained relationships, and a lack of trust from others.

To cultivate true confidence and avoid falling into the trap of cockiness, it's essential to practice self-awareness, humility, and empathy. Take time to reflect on your strengths and weaknesses and be honest with yourself about areas where you need to grow and improve. Celebrate your accomplishments, but also acknowledge the contributions and successes of others.

Surround yourself with supportive, honest individuals who can provide constructive feedback and help you maintain a realistic perspective. Practice active listening and look to understand the experiences and viewpoints of those around you. By approaching others with respect, kindness, and a willingness to learn, you can build genuine, lasting connections and create a positive impact in your personal and professional life.

While confidence and cockiness may appear similar on the surface, they are fundamentally different qualities. Confidence is a positive, healthy trait that empowers individuals to pursue their goals, overcome challenges, and inspire others, while cockiness is a negative, self-serving attitude that can hinder personal growth and damage relationships. By cultivating true confidence through self-awareness, humility, and empathy, you can unlock your full potential and create a life of purpose, fulfillment, and genuine connection.

Why Confidence is Good and Being Cocky Will Always Hold You Back

Confidence is a valuable and desirable trait that can have a profound impact on every aspect of your life. When you own genuine self-assurance, you are better equipped to pursue your goals, overcome obstacles, and create meaningful connections with others. Confidence allows you to trust in your abilities, take calculated risks, and bounce back from setbacks with resilience and determination.

One of the most significant benefits of confidence is that it enables you to step outside your comfort zone and seize new opportunities. When you believe in yourself and your capabilities, you are more likely to take on challenges that others may shy away from, leading to personal and professional growth. Confident individuals are not afraid to speak up, share their ideas, and advocate for themselves and others, creating positive change in their lives and communities.

Confidence also plays a crucial role in building strong, healthy relationships. When you are secure in yourself, you are better able to communicate openly and honestly with others, set healthy boundaries, and foster a sense of trust and respect. Confident individuals are more likely to approach others with empathy and kindness, creating a positive and supportive environment that encourages growth and collaboration.

Moreover, confidence is attractive and inspiring to others. When you exude self-assurance, you naturally draw people to you and inspire them to believe in themselves and their own abilities. By serving as a role model of confidence, you can help others cultivate their own self-assurance and create a ripple effect of positivity and empowerment.

In contrast, being cocky can have detrimental effects on your personal and professional life. Cockiness is often rooted in insecurity and a need for external validation, leading individuals to engage in self-serving and arrogant behavior. Cocky people may boast about their accomplishments, belittle the efforts of others, and prioritize their own needs and desires over those of others.

This type of behavior can quickly alienate others and damage relationships. Cocky individuals may struggle to form genuine connections, as their arrogance and lack of empathy can be off-putting and hurtful to those around them. They may also have difficulty collaborating with others or accepting constructive feedback, hindering their ability to learn, grow, and improve.

Cockiness can lead to poor decision-making and risky behavior. When individuals overestimate their abilities or underestimate potential challenges, they may take unnecessary risks or not consider the consequences of their actions. This can result in personal and professional setbacks, financial losses, and a damaged reputation.

Cockiness can also limit personal and professional growth. When individuals believe they already know everything or have nothing left to learn, they miss valuable opportunities to expand their knowledge, skills, and perspectives. This narrow-minded approach can lead to stagnation and a lack of progress, both personally and professionally.

To avoid the pitfalls of cockiness and cultivate genuine confidence, it's essential to practice humility, self-awareness, and a willingness to learn. Embrace the fact that there is always room for growth and improvement and seek out opportunities to challenge yourself and expand your horizons. Surround yourself with individuals who provide honest, constructive feedback and support your personal and professional development.

Remember, true confidence is not about being perfect or having all the answers. It's about believing in yourself, your abilities, and your potential to learn, grow, and overcome challenges. By focusing on building genuine self-assurance, you can create a life of purpose, fulfillment, and positive impact, while avoiding the negative consequences of cockiness.

Confidence is a valuable and essential trait that can transform your life in countless positive ways, while cockiness is a destructive and limiting quality that can hold you back from reaching your full potential. By cultivating true confidence through humility, self-awareness, and a commitment to personal growth, you can unlock your inner strength, build meaningful relationships, and create a life of purpose and success.

Chapter 8: List of most successful people that are or were confident!

Here are the top 50 extraordinarily successful and confident individuals from various fields, along with a brief description of what they do or did:

1. Oprah Winfrey - Media mogul, actress, and philanthropist

2. Elon Musk - Entrepreneur, CEO of Tesla and SpaceX

3. Steve Jobs (1955-2011) - Co-founder and former CEO of Apple Inc.

4. Jeff Bezos - Founder and Executive Chairman of Amazon

5. Warren Buffett - Investor, business tycoon, and philanthropist

6. Bill Gates - Co-founder of Microsoft, investor, and philanthropist

7. Barack Obama - 44th President of the United States

8. Michelle Obama - Former First Lady, lawyer, and author

9. Sheryl Sandberg - Chief Operating Officer of Facebook (Meta)

10. Richard Branson - Founder of Virgin Group

11. Indra Nooyi - Former CEO of PepsiCo

12. Arianna Huffington - Co-founder of The Huffington Post and founder of Thrive Global

13. Mark Zuckerberg - Co-founder and CEO of Facebook (Meta)

14. Serena Williams - Professional tennis player and entrepreneur

15. LeBron James - Professional basketball player and philanthropist

16. Beyoncé Knowles - Singer, songwriter, record producer, and actress

17. Jay-Z - Rapper, record producer, and entrepreneur

18. Angela Merkel - Former Chancellor of Germany

19. Ruth Bader Ginsburg (1933-2020) - Former Associate Justice of the U.S. Supreme Court

20. Malala Yousafzai - Activist, youngest Nobel Prize laureate

21. Satya Nadella - CEO of Microsoft

22. Jacinda Ardern - Prime Minister of New Zealand

23. Shonda Rhimes - Television producer, screenwriter, and author

24. Sundar Pichai - CEO of Alphabet Inc. and Google

25. Kamala Harris - Vice President of the United States

26. Melinda Gates - Philanthropist and former General Manager at Microsoft

27. Ursula Burns - Former CEO of Xerox and current Chairman of VEON

28. Mary Barra - CEO of General Motors

29. Ginni Rometty - Former CEO and Executive Chairman of IBM

30. Meg Whitman - Former CEO of Hewlett Packard Enterprise and current U.S. Ambassador to Kenya

31. Jamie Dimon - Chairman and CEO of JPMorgan Chase

32. Abigail Johnson - President and CEO of Fidelity Investments

33. Mukesh Ambani - Chairman and Managing Director of Reliance Industries

34. Jack Ma - Co-founder and former Executive Chairman of Alibaba Group

35. Tim Cook - CEO of Apple Inc.

36. Dwayne "The Rock" Johnson - Actor, producer, and former professional wrestler

37. Cristiano Ronaldo - Professional soccer player and entrepreneur

38. Rihanna - Singer, actress, and businesswoman

39. Angelina Jolie - Actress, filmmaker, and humanitarian

40. Leonardo DiCaprio - Actor, producer, and environmentalist

41. Meryl Streep - Actress and philanthropist

42. Steven Spielberg - Filmmaker and co-founder of DreamWorks Studios

43. J.K. Rowling - Author of the Harry Potter series and philanthropist

44. Kimberly Bryant - Founder of Black Girls Code

45. Reed Hastings - Co-founder, Chairman, and co-CEO of Netflix

46. Marissa Mayer - Former CEO of Yahoo! and co-founder of Sunshine

47. Reshma Saujani - Founder and CEO of Girls Who Code

48. Adena Friedman - President and CEO of Nasdaq

49. Drew Faust - Former President of Harvard University

50. Jacqueline Novogratz - Founder and CEO of Acumen

These individuals have demonstrated confidence, leadership, and success in their respective fields, ranging from business and technology to politics, entertainment, activism, and education.

My advice. Repeat to yourself everyday..."I CAN DO ANYTHING"

My advice to you, whether you are a man, woman, teenager, or child, is simple yet powerful: Repeat to yourself every day, "I CAN DO ANYTHING." These four words have the ability to transform your mindset, boost your confidence, and propel you towards achieving your goals.

Confidence is key in every aspect of life. It is the belief in yourself and your abilities that allows you to take risks, overcome challenges, and reach your full potential. By affirming to yourself that you can do anything, you are instilling a sense of empowerment and self-assurance that will carry you through even the toughest of times.

When you repeat this mantra daily, you are programming your subconscious mind to believe in your capabilities. You are training yourself to think positively, to push past self-doubt, and to embrace challenges as opportunities for growth.

Whether you are facing a challenging task at work, navigating a new relationship, or pursuing a personal passion, reminding yourself that you can do anything will give you the courage and determination to succeed. It will remind you that you are capable, resilient, and worthy of all the success that comes your way.

So, take a moment each day to look in the mirror and repeat these words to yourself. Let them sink into your soul and guide you on your journey towards fearlessness and confidence. Remember, you CAN do anything. Believe it, live it, and watch as your life transforms before your eyes.

RELEASING YOUR INNER WARRIOR

Chapter 9: Introduction to Unleashing Your Inner Warrior

The Power of Embracing Challenges

Life is a battle, and every individual faces their own unique set of challenges. Whether it be personal struggles, professional obstacles, or societal pressures, the path to success is often paved with hardships. However, it is through embracing these challenges that we can truly unleash our inner warrior and master the art of conquering life's battles.

Challenges are not meant to break us; they are meant to build us. They provide us with opportunities to grow, learn, and transform into stronger versions of ourselves. When we choose to confront our challenges head-on, we tap into a wellspring of resilience, determination, and courage that we may not have known existed within us.

One of the most powerful ways to embrace challenges is by shifting our mindset. Instead of viewing obstacles as insurmountable roadblocks, we can choose to see them as steppingstones towards personal growth and self-improvement. By reframing our perspective, we open ourselves up to new possibilities and invite the potential for positive change into our lives.

Embracing challenges also requires us to step out of our comfort zones. Growth and progress rarely occur within the confines of familiarity. By willingly stepping into the unknown, we stretch our limits, explore our capabilities, and discover hidden strengths we never knew we had. It is through these experiences that we cultivate resilience and build the mental fortitude necessary to face any battle that comes our way.

Moreover, embracing challenges allows us to develop a sense of empowerment. When we take control of our circumstances and refuse to be defined by our struggles, we reclaim our power and become the architects of our destiny. We understand that challenges do not define us; rather, it is our response to them that shapes our character and determines our ultimate success.

In the journey of life, challenges are inevitable. However, it is our choice whether we allow them to hinder our progress or become catalysts for growth. By embracing challenges, we tap into our inner warrior and unlock our true potential. We become unstoppable forces, capable of conquering any battle that comes our way.

So, to all people facing the battles of life, remember that challenges are not meant to break you. Embrace them, for they hold the keys to your personal growth, empowerment, and success. Embrace them and unleash your inner warrior. You have the power to conquer anything that comes your way.

Understanding Your Inner Warrior

In the journey of life, we all face battles. Whether they are external challenges or internal struggles, we constantly find ourselves during a life battle. However, within each of us lies a powerful force that can help us conquer these challenges – our inner warrior.

But who is this inner warrior, and how can we understand and unleash its power? The concept of the inner warrior goes beyond physical strength or combat skills. It encompasses the mental, emotional, and spiritual fortitude that enables us to face adversity head-on and appear victorious.

To tap into the power of your inner warrior, you must first recognize its existence. It is the part of you that refuses to give up, that pushes through when the odds are against you. It is that voice inside that says, "I can do this," even when everything seems impossible. Understanding your inner warrior means acknowledging that you have the strength, resilience, and determination to overcome any obstacle that comes your way.

One key aspect of understanding your inner warrior is honing your self-awareness. Take the time to reflect on your strengths, weaknesses, and values. Name what motivates you and what holds you back. Understanding your inner warrior requires embracing your authentic self and acknowledging both your light and dark sides.

Additionally, nurturing a positive mindset is essential in unleashing your inner warrior. Cultivate an attitude of resilience, optimism, and gratitude. Embrace challenges as opportunities for growth and view failures as steppingstones towards success. By adopting a positive mindset, you can transform obstacles into steppingstones on your journey towards conquering life's challenges.

Furthermore, understanding your inner warrior involves developing a deep sense of purpose. Clarify your goals, passions, and values, and align your actions with them. When you have a clear sense of purpose, you become unstoppable. Your inner warrior is fueled by a burning desire to make a difference and leave a positive impact on the world.

Remember, the life battle is not about avoiding challenges but rather about embracing them and growing through them. Your inner warrior is your greatest ally in this battle. By understanding and acknowledging its power, you can unleash your full potential and master the art of conquering life's challenges.

Understanding your inner warrior is a transformative process that allows you to harness your inner strength and navigate life's battles with confidence and resilience. By embracing your authentic self, cultivating a positive mindset, and aligning with your purpose, you can unleash the power within you and become the master of your own destiny. So, step into the arena and let your inner warrior guide you towards a life filled with triumph and fulfillment.

Chapter 10: Building a Strong Foundation

Cultivating a Positive Mindset

In the battle of life, our mindset is our greatest weapon. How we approach challenges and setbacks can figure out the outcome of our journey. In this subchapter, we will explore the importance of cultivating a positive mindset and how it can help us conquer life's challenges.

A positive mindset is a state of mind that enables us to see the positive aspect in every situation. It is about focusing on the possibilities rather than dwelling on the limitations. When we cultivate a positive mindset, we train our minds to see opportunities in adversity, to believe in our abilities, and to approach life with an unwavering optimism.

One of the first steps in cultivating a positive mindset is to practice gratitude. By recognizing and appreciating the blessings in our lives, we shift our focus from what is lacking to what is abundant. Gratitude allows us to find strength and joy even amid difficult circumstances. It reminds us of the power of perspective and helps us keep a positive outlook.

Another aspect of cultivating a positive mindset is developing a growth mindset. This mindset embraces challenges as opportunities for growth and learning. Instead of fearing failure, we see it as a steppingstone towards success. By adopting a growth mindset, we become more resilient, adaptable, and open to new possibilities.

Positive self-talk is also crucial in cultivating a positive mindset. The way we speak to ourselves can either lift us up or bring us down. By replacing negative thoughts with positive affirmations, we can rewire our brains to focus on our strengths and potential. This practice not only boosts our self-confidence but also enhances our overall well-being.

Surrounding ourselves with positive influences is another key part of cultivating a positive mindset. The people we spend time with greatly impact our thoughts and beliefs. By surrounding ourselves with individuals who uplift and inspire us, we create an environment that fosters positivity and personal growth.

Cultivating a positive mindset is essential in conquering life's challenges. By practicing gratitude, adopting a growth mindset, engaging in positive self-talk, and surrounding ourselves with positive influences, we empower ourselves to overcome obstacles and embrace the journey of life with resilience and optimism. Remember, your mindset is your greatest weapon in the battle of life. Choose positivity, and you will unleash your inner warrior.

Developing Self-Confidence

In the battlefield of life, self-confidence is the armor that can protect us from the blows of self-doubt and insecurity. It is the foundation upon which we can build a successful and fulfilling life. Self-confidence is not something we are born with, but rather a skill that can be developed and nurtured over time. In this subchapter, we will explore the various strategies and techniques to unleash and cultivate your inner warrior of self-confidence.

The first step towards developing self-confidence is to understand and accept oneself. Embrace your strengths and weaknesses, for they make you unique. Acknowledge your accomplishments and learn from your failures. By recognizing your worth and potential, you lay the groundwork for self-belief.

Another important aspect of building self-confidence is setting and achieving goals. Break down your aspirations into smaller, manageable steps and celebrate every milestone along the way. By taking consistent action towards your goals, you prove to yourself that you are capable of success.

A positive mindset is crucial in developing self-confidence. Challenge negative thoughts and replace them with positive affirmations. Surround yourself with supportive and encouraging individuals who believe in your abilities. Remember, you are the average of the people you surround yourself with, so choose wisely.

Fear is the mortal enemy of self-confidence. To conquer fear, you must face it head-on. Take calculated risks and step outside of your comfort zone. Each time you overcome a fear, your self-confidence grows stronger, and you become more resilient in the face of adversity.

Self-care plays a significant role in developing self-confidence. Prioritize your physical and mental well-being. Exercise regularly, eat a balanced diet, and get enough rest. Engage in activities that bring you joy and relaxation. By taking care of yourself, you send a powerful message to your subconscious that you matter.

Lastly, practice self-compassion. Treat yourself with kindness and forgiveness, just as you would a dear friend. Accept that mistakes are a part of the learning process and use them as steppingstones towards growth. Self-compassion allows you to bounce back from setbacks and maintain a positive self-image.

Developing self-confidence is an ongoing journey that requires patience, persistence, and self-reflection. By embracing your uniqueness, setting goals, cultivating a positive mindset, facing your fears, practicing self-care, and showing self-compassion, you can unleash your inner warrior and conquer the battles of life with unwavering confidence. Remember, you can achieve greatness – believe in yourself, and the world will believe in you.

Setting Goals for Success

In order to conquer life's challenges and emerge victorious in the battle of life, it is crucial to set goals for success. Setting goals not only provides direction and purpose but also serves as a powerful motivator to keep pushing forward. Whether you are fighting personal battles, professional challenges, or seeking overall self-improvement, proving clear and achievable goals can be the key to unlocking your inner warrior.

Goals act as a roadmap, guiding us towards our desired destination. Without a clear target in mind, we may find ourselves wandering aimlessly, lacking focus and direction. When we set goals, we create a sense of purpose and develop a strategic plan to overcome obstacles and achieve our desired outcomes.

To set effective goals, it is important to follow a few key principles. Firstly, goals should be specific and measurable. Vague aspirations such as "I want to be successful" or "I want to be happy" lack clarity and make it difficult to track progress. Instead, define your goals in precise terms and prove measurable criteria to evaluate your achievements.

Additionally, goals should be realistic and attainable. While it is important to dream big, setting unrealistic goals can lead to disappointment and demotivation. Break your larger goals into smaller, achievable milestones to make your journey towards success more manageable and less overwhelming.

Moreover, setting a timeline for your goals is essential. Deadlines create a sense of urgency and prevent procrastination. By setting specific periods, you hold yourself accountable and create a sense of discipline that propels you towards success.

It is crucial to regularly review and adjust your goals. Life is dynamic, and circumstances change. By reassessing your goals periodically, you can adapt to new challenges and opportunities, ensuring that your goals still are relevant and aligned with your evolving aspirations.

Setting goals for success is a fundamental step in conquering life's battles. By showing clear and achievable goals, you provide yourself with direction, motivation, and a roadmap towards victory. Remember to make your goals specific, measurable, realistic, and time-bound, allowing you to track progress, stay focused, and adjust as needed. With a strong goal-setting framework in place, you can unleash your inner warrior and master the art of conquering life's challenges.

Chapter 11: Harnessing Your Inner Strength

Identifying and Utilizing Your Strengths

Chapter X: Identifying and Utilizing Your Strengths

In the battlefield of life, where challenges lurk around every corner, it is crucial to be armed with a deep understanding of our own strengths. Each one of us has unique qualities and abilities that can help us conquer the battles we face. The subchapter "Identifying and Utilizing Your Strengths" in our book, "Unleashing Your Inner Warrior: Mastering the Art of Conquering Life's Challenges," is dedicated to helping all people, regardless of their background or circumstances, discover and harness their inner power.

The first step towards finding your strengths is self-reflection. Take a moment to ponder on your accomplishments, both big and small. What are the skills, qualities, or traits that have helped you overcome obstacles in the past? Perhaps you have a knack for problem-solving, an intense sense of empathy, or an unwavering determination. Acknowledge and celebrate these strengths, as they are the building blocks of your success.

It is also essential to seek feedback from others. Reach out to friends, family, mentors, or colleagues and ask them about the qualities they admire in you. Often, we are unaware of our own strengths, and the perspectives of others can shed light on our unique abilities. Embrace their feedback and use it to gain a comprehensive understanding of your strengths.

Once you have found your strengths, it is time to use them effectively. Imagine your strengths as tools in a warrior's arsenal. Just as a skilled warrior strategically selects the right weapon for each battle, you must learn to apply your strengths in the most helpful way. For instance, if you excel at problem-solving, use this skill to tackle complex challenges head-on. If you have an empathetic nature, use it to build strong relationships and support others on their journey.

However, it is important to remember that strengths alone do not guarantee victory. Your strengths must be honed and refined through continuous learning and practice. Seek opportunities to further develop your strengths, whether through formal education, mentorship, or real-life experiences. By investing time and effort into your strengths, you will transform them into formidable assets that can overcome even the toughest of challenges.

Identifying and using your strengths is a fundamental aspect of mastering life's battles. By engaging in self-reflection, seeking feedback, and honing your abilities, you can harness your inner power and conquer any obstacle that comes your way. Remember, each one of us has unique strengths - the key lies in recognizing them and deploying them strategically. Embrace your strengths, unleash your inner warrior, and triumph over life's challenges.

Overcoming Limiting Beliefs

In the battlefield of life, we often find ourselves facing formidable opponents. These adversaries may not be physical in nature, but they can be just as powerful and debilitating – our own limiting beliefs. These self-imposed barriers prevent us from reaching our full potential and hinder us from conquering life's challenges. However, with the right mindset and strategies, we can overcome these limiting beliefs and unleash our inner warrior.

Limiting beliefs are those deeply ingrained thoughts and beliefs we hold about ourselves and the world around us that restrict our actions and potential. They are formed over time and reinforced by negative experiences, societal expectations, and our own self-doubt. These beliefs convince us that we are not capable, worthy, or deserving of success and happiness. They tell us that we are too old, too young, or too inexperienced to achieve greatness.

To overcome these limiting beliefs, we must first become aware of them. Self-reflection and introspection are vital in this process. Ask yourself: What beliefs have been holding me back? What stories have I been telling myself? Once you find these limiting beliefs, challenge them. Question their validity and seek evidence to counter them. Replace them with empowering beliefs that align with your true potential.

Another powerful tool in overcoming limiting beliefs is visualization. Envision yourself overcoming obstacles, achieving your goals, and living your best life. This practice rewires your brain, creating new neural pathways that reinforce positive beliefs and behaviors. Combine visualization with affirmations – positive statements that affirm your capabilities and strengths. Repeat these affirmations daily, internalizing them until they become your truth.

Surrounding yourself with a supportive network is equally important. Seek out mentors, coaches, or like-minded individuals who can provide guidance, encouragement, and accountability. Sharing your journey with others who have conquered their own limiting beliefs can inspire and motivate you to do the same.

Taking consistent action is the final and most crucial step in overcoming limiting beliefs. Break down your goals into smaller, manageable tasks and take concrete steps towards achieving them. Celebrate each small victory along the way, building momentum and confidence. Remember that success is not linear, and setbacks are a natural part of the journey. Embrace them as opportunities for growth and learning, rather than validation of your limiting beliefs.

In the battle of life, overcoming limiting beliefs is essential for victory. By cultivating self-awareness, challenging negative beliefs, visualizing success, building a support system, and taking consistent action, you can unleash your inner warrior and conquer life's challenges. Remember, you are stronger than you think, and your potential knows no bounds. It's time to break free from the shackles of limiting beliefs and embrace the warrior within you.

Embracing Resilience and Adaptability

Life is an unpredictable journey, filled with countless battles that we must face and conquer. Whether it's overcoming personal hardships, professional setbacks, or unexpected obstacles, the ability to embrace resilience and adaptability becomes crucial in our quest for success and fulfillment. In this subchapter of "Unleashing Your Inner Warrior: Mastering the Art of Conquering Life's Challenges," we delve into the essence of resilience and adaptability and how they can empower us to navigate "THE LIFE BATTLE."

Resilience is the unwavering strength that lies within us, enabling us to bounce back from adversity with renewed determination. It is the ability to see setbacks as opportunities for growth rather than insurmountable barriers. Resilience allows us to overcome obstacles, learn from our failures, and appear stronger and more resilient than ever before. By embracing resilience, we develop the mental fortitude to persevere through life's challenges and come out on top.

Adaptability, on the other hand, is the art of being flexible and open to change. In a world that is constantly evolving, adaptability becomes a vital skill that empowers us to thrive amidst uncertainty. It requires us to be proactive, open-minded, and willing to step outside our comfort zones. By embracing adaptability, we become better equipped to navigate through the twists and turns that life presents us, adjusting our strategies and approaches as needed.

When we combine resilience and adaptability, we unlock the true potential of our inner warrior. It is through embracing these qualities that we can transform setbacks into learning, failures into opportunities, and uncertainty into growth. By cultivating resilience and adaptability, we become better equipped to face THE LIFE BATTLE head-on, appearing not only victorious but also transformed.

In this subchapter, you will discover practical strategies and techniques to strengthen your resilience and adaptability. From developing a growth mindset to mastering the art of problem-solving, each page will guide you towards unleashing your inner warrior. Through inspiring stories and insightful exercises, you will learn how to embrace resilience and adaptability, equipping yourself with the tools needed to conquer life's challenges.

This subchapter is dedicated to all people who are navigating THE LIFE BATTLE and looking to unleash their inner warrior. Whether you are a student, professional, or homemaker, the lessons within these pages are universal and applicable to all occupations. Embrace resilience and adaptability and embark on a transformative journey towards conquering life's challenges with unwavering strength and unyielding determination.

Chapter 12: Mastering Self-Discipline and Motivation

Cultivating Self-Discipline

In the battlefield of life, where challenges constantly arise, cultivating self-discipline is an essential skill that can transform you into a true warrior. Regardless of your background, age, or circumstances, the ability to conquer life's challenges lies within your own self-discipline. This subchapter will guide you on your journey to unlocking the power of self-discipline, enabling you to overcome any obstacle that stands in your way.

Self-discipline is the cornerstone of personal growth and success. It is the ability to control your thoughts, emotions, and actions in pursuit of your goals and dreams. Without self-discipline, you may find yourself drifting aimlessly, unable to stay focused or committed to your aspirations. However, by mastering this art, you will become the captain of your own destiny, capable of achieving greatness in every aspect of your life.

One of the key principles in cultivating self-discipline is setting clear and specific goals. Without a target to aim for, you may find yourself easily sidetracked or overwhelmed. By defining your goals and breaking them down into smaller, actionable steps, you create a roadmap for success. This clarity helps to strengthen your self-discipline, as you can measure your progress and stay motivated along the way.

Another important aspect of self-discipline is the ability to delay gratification. In an instant gratification society, it is easy to be tempted by short-term pleasures that hinder long-term progress. However, as a warrior of life, you understand the power of delayed gratification. By resisting instant gratification and focusing on the bigger picture, you can make choices that align with your long-term goals, ultimately leading to greater fulfillment and success.

Furthermore, cultivating self-discipline requires developing strong habits and routines. By incorporating positive habits into your daily life, you create a structure that supports your growth and discipline. Whether it's waking up early, exercising regularly, or practicing mindfulness, these habits reinforce your commitment to self-discipline and empower you to face life's challenges head-on.

Remember, self-discipline is not an innate trait but a skill that can be learned and strengthened over time. It requires consistent practice, dedication, and perseverance. The journey towards cultivating self-discipline may not always be easy, but the rewards are immeasurable. By mastering this art, you will unleash your inner warrior and become unstoppable in conquering life's battles.

So, embrace the power of self-discipline, set your goals, delay gratification, and show empowering habits. With each step, you will inch closer to unlocking your true potential and living a life of fulfillment and triumph. Let your inner warrior guide you, as you cultivate the self-discipline necessary to conquer any challenge that comes your way.

Finding and Sustaining Motivation

Motivation is the driving force behind all our actions. It is what propels us forward, even in the face of adversity, and keeps us going when we want to give up. In the battleground of life, where challenges are abundant and victory is hard-fought, finding and sustaining motivation becomes paramount. This subchapter will explore the key principles and strategies to unleash your inner warrior and conquer life's challenges.

Motivation is not a constant state; it ebbs and flows. At times, it may seem elusive, but by understanding the factors that influence our motivation, we can learn how to harness its power. One of the first steps in finding motivation is finding your purpose or the driving force behind your actions. What is it that truly inspires and ignites your passion? Reflect on your values, goals, and dreams to uncover what truly motivates you in life.

Once you have named your motivation, the next step is to create a roadmap to sustain it. This involves setting clear and achievable goals. Break down your larger goals into smaller, more manageable steps and celebrate each milestone along the way. By tracking your progress, you will stay motivated as you see your growth and accomplishments.

It is important to surround yourself with positive influences and a supportive community. Connect with like-minded individuals who share similar goals and aspirations. Engage in conversations, attend workshops, or join online communities that foster growth and motivation. By surrounding yourself with people who believe in you and your journey, you will find the strength and encouragement to push through even the toughest of challenges.

Another powerful tool to sustain motivation is visualization. Take time each day to visualize yourself overcoming obstacles and achieving your goals. Imagine the feelings of success and accomplishment. This visualization exercise will reinforce your motivation and keep your focus aligned with your desired outcomes.

Inevitably, there will be setbacks and moments of doubt. During these challenging times, it is crucial to practice self-compassion and self-care. Remind yourself that setbacks are part of the journey, and mistakes are opportunities for growth. Take care of your physical, emotional, and mental well-being by engaging in activities that recharge and rejuvenate you.

Remember, motivation is not a finite resource. It is a skill that can be developed and nurtured. By understanding what motivates you, setting clear goals, surrounding yourself with positive influences, visualizing success, and practicing self-care, you can unleash your inner warrior and conquer life's battles.

In the end, it is your commitment and dedication to finding and sustaining motivation that will ultimately lead you to triumph. Embrace the challenges, stay focused on your goals, and let your inner warrior shine. The journey may not be easy, but with unwavering motivation, you can conquer anything life throws your way.

Creating Effective Habits

In the battle of life, it is essential to equip ourselves with powerful tools that can help us conquer the challenges that come our way. One of the most potent weapons we possess is the ability to create effective habits. Habits, whether good or bad, shape our lives and determine our success. In this subchapter, we will explore the art of creating effective habits and how they can transform us into warriors who conquer life's battles.

To begin, let's understand what makes a habit effective. An effective habit is one that aligns with our goals, values, and aspirations. It is a behavior or routine that propels us forward, rather than holding us back. Effective habits are built upon discipline, consistency, and a growth mindset.

The first step in creating effective habits is to identify our goals. What do we want to achieve in life? What battles are we fighting? Once we have an unobstructed vision of our goals, we can design habits that support them. For example, if our battle is to improve our physical fitness, we can create a habit of exercising daily or eating a balanced diet.

Consistency is key when it comes to building effective habits. It takes time and effort to make a habit stick. Research suggests that it takes an average of 66 days for a behavior to become automatic. Therefore, it is crucial to commit to our habits for an extended period, despite any challenges or setbacks we may encounter along the way.

Another essential aspect of creating effective habits is to cultivate a growth mindset. We must believe that we have the potential to change and improve. Embracing a growth mindset allows us to view setbacks as opportunities for growth rather than failures. It enables us to learn from our mistakes and persevere in the face of adversity.

To reinforce our habits, it helps to create an environment that supports our goals. Surrounding ourselves with like-minded individuals, seeking accountability partners, or changing our physical surroundings can all contribute to the success of our habits.

Creating effective habits is a fundamental skill for conquering life's battles. By aligning our habits with our goals, staying consistent, and embracing a growth mindset, we can unleash our inner warrior and overcome any challenge that comes our way. Remember, the power to transform our lives lies in our hands. Let us seize it by creating effective habits and becoming the warriors we were meant to be.

Chapter 13: Navigating through Adversity

Developing Problem-Solving Skills

In the battlefield of life, challenges and obstacles are inevitable. Whether you are facing personal struggles, professional dilemmas, or societal issues, the ability to solve problems effectively is essential. This subchapter will guide all people, regardless of their background or circumstances, in developing and mastering problem-solving skills to conquer life's challenges.

Problem-solving skills are not innate; they can be learned and honed through practice and dedication. By cultivating these skills, you will gain the confidence and resilience needed to overcome any obstacle that comes your way. Here are some key strategies to unleash your inner warrior and become a master problem solver:

1. Embrace a Growth Mindset: Adopting a growth mindset is crucial in problem-solving. Believe that challenges are opportunities for growth and learning. View setbacks as stepping stones towards success rather than roadblocks.

2. Analyze the Problem: Break down the problem into smaller, manageable parts. Understand the root cause and show any underlying factors contributing to

the issue. This step helps you gain clarity and develop a strategic approach.

3. Think Creatively: Encourage yourself to think freely. Explore different perspectives and consider unconventional solutions. Embrace creativity and innovation as powerful tools to tackle complex problems.

4. Seek Collaborative Solutions: Recognize that problem-solving does not have to be a solitary endeavor. Engage with others who may offer diverse insights and ability. Collaborative problem-solving fosters teamwork and strengthens relationships.

5. Implement Action Plans: Once you have named a solution, create a detailed action plan. Break down the steps needed to implement your solution and provide a timeline. This will help you stay organized and focused throughout the problem-solving process.

6. Learn from Mistakes: Understand that setbacks and failures are part of the problem-solving journey. Embrace them as opportunities to learn and grow. Reflect on your experiences, identify areas for improvement, and adjust your approach accordingly.

7. Adapt and Iterate: Problem-solving is an iterative process. Be flexible and willing to adapt your strategies as current information arises. Embrace change and continuously refine your approach to ensure long-term success.

By developing problem-solving skills, you equip yourself with the tools to triumph over life's battles.

Remember, every challenge you face is an opportunity for growth and self-discovery. Embrace these skills and unleash your inner warrior to conquer whatever obstacles may come your way. With dedication, resilience, and a growth mindset, you can overcome any challenge and emerge victorious in THE LIFE BATTLE.

Overcoming Obstacles and Roadblocks

Life is full of challenges and obstacles that often stand in the way of our dreams and goals. Whether it is a personal struggle, a professional setback, or a demanding situation, we all face roadblocks that test our resilience and determination. However, it is in these moments of adversity that our true strength and inner warrior can appear.

In the subchapter of "Unleashing Your Inner Warrior: Mastering the Art of Conquering Life's Challenges" titled "Overcoming Obstacles and Roadblocks," we delve into strategies and mindset shifts that can empower all people in their life battles. Regardless of your background, age, or circumstances, this chapter serves as a guide to help you navigate through the toughest of challenges and come out stronger on the other side.

One of the fundamental principles we explore is the power of mindset. When faced with a roadblock, it is essential to shift our perspective and view it as an opportunity for growth and learning. By reframing obstacles as on our journey, we can tap into our inner warrior and adopt a solution-oriented mindset. This perspective allows us to embrace challenges, learn from them, and find creative ways to overcome them.

Another crucial aspect we delve into is the importance of resilience. Life is not always smooth sailing, and setbacks are inevitable. However, it is our ability to bounce back and persevere that differentiates those who succeed from those who give up. We provide practical tools and techniques to build resilience, such as developing a support network, practicing self-care, and cultivating a positive mindset.

Furthermore, we emphasize the significance of self-belief and the power of self-talk. Overcoming obstacles often requires us to push past our comfort zones and confront our fears. By cultivating a belief in our abilities and adopting positive self-talk, we can conquer self-doubt and take bold steps towards our goals.

Throughout this subchapter, we share inspiring stories of individuals who have triumphed over tremendous obstacles – individuals who have proven that the human spirit is capable of incredible feats. These stories serve as a reminder that no matter how insurmountable a roadblock may appear, there is always a way forward.

"Overcoming Obstacles and Roadblocks" is not just a subchapter; it is a roadmap to unlocking your inner warrior and conquering life's challenges. Whether you are facing personal struggles, professional setbacks, or simply seeking inspiration to navigate the difficulties of life, this chapter is for you. Embrace the power within, unleash your inner warrior, and embark on a journey of resilience, growth, and triumph.

Embracing Change and Uncertainty

Change and uncertainty are inevitable aspects of life. We all face various battles and challenges throughout our journey, and it is our ability to embrace change and uncertainty that determines our success in conquering them. In this subchapter, we explore the importance of developing a mindset that thrives in the face of uncertainty, enabling us to unleash our inner warrior and master the art of conquering life's challenges.

Life is a constant ebb and flow, and resisting change only hinders our growth. Instead, we must learn to adapt and embrace new circumstances, even when they seem daunting. Embracing change allows us to open ourselves up to new opportunities and experiences that can shape our lives for the better. By accepting change as an inevitable part of life, we become more resilient and capable of navigating through the unknown.

Uncertainty often brings fear and anxiety, but it is during these times that we truly discover our inner strength. Rather than allowing uncertainty to paralyze us, we can choose to see it as a catalyst for growth and personal development. Embracing uncertainty means stepping outside of our comfort zones and challenging ourselves to explore the unknown. It is in these moments of uncertainty that we have the opportunity to learn, grow, and evolve.

To embrace change and uncertainty, we must cultivate a mindset of curiosity and adaptability. Instead of resisting change, we can approach it with an open mind, looking to understand its potential benefits. By reframing our perspective, we can transform change into an opportunity for growth and self-improvement.

Moreover, embracing change and uncertainty requires us to let go of the need for control. Accepting that we cannot control every aspect of our lives allows us to surrender to the flow of life and trust in the process. It is through this surrender that we find peace and the ability to navigate through life's challenges with grace.

Embracing change and uncertainty is essential for conquering life's battles. By developing a mindset that welcomes change and thrives in uncertainty, we unlock our inner warrior and tap into our true potential. When we embrace change, we open ourselves up to new possibilities and experiences. When we embrace uncertainty, we discover our inner strength and resilience. So let us embrace change and uncertainty, for it is through these moments that we truly conquer life's challenges and unleash our inner warrior.

Chapter 14: The Warrior's Mindset

Cultivating Mental Toughness

In the battlefield of life, we often find ourselves facing numerous challenges that test our mental and emotional fortitude. It is during these moments that cultivating mental toughness becomes crucial to overcome obstacles and emerge victorious. Mental toughness is not a trait that we are born with, but rather a skill that can be developed and honed over time. In this subchapter, we will dive deep into the art of cultivating mental toughness, equipping you with the tools and strategies needed to conquer life's challenges.

One of the fundamental aspects of cultivating mental toughness is developing a resilient mindset. Resilience allows us to bounce back from setbacks, view failures as learning opportunities, and maintain a positive outlook even in the face of adversity. By reframing our thoughts and focusing on solutions rather than dwelling on problems, we can build mental resilience and develop the ability to persevere.

Another key aspect of mental toughness is self-discipline. It is the ability to stay focused and committed to our goals, even when distractions abound. By practicing self-discipline, we can cultivate the mental strength needed to resist temptations, maintain healthy habits, and stay on track despite the challenges that arise.

Moreover, cultivating mental toughness also involves managing stress and controlling our emotions. Stress can often cloud our judgment and hinder our ability to make rational decisions. By implementing stress management techniques such as deep breathing exercises, meditation, and regular physical activity, we can reduce stress levels and maintain a clear and focused mind.

Additionally, it is crucial to develop a growth mindset, which involves embracing challenges, persisting in the face of setbacks, and seeking opportunities for personal growth and development. By cultivating a growth mindset, we can view obstacles as stepping stones towards success, rather than insurmountable roadblocks.

Lastly, building a support system and surrounding ourselves with positive influences can significantly contribute to our mental toughness. Connecting with like-minded individuals who share our goals and aspirations can provide invaluable support, encouragement, and motivation during challenging times.

Cultivating mental toughness is a lifelong journey that requires dedication, perseverance, and a willingness to step out of our comfort zones. By developing a resilient mindset, practicing self-discipline, managing stress, embracing challenges, and building a strong support system, we can unleash our inner warrior and conquer life's battles with unwavering determination and strength. Remember, mental toughness is not about being invincible; it is about having the courage to persist and rise above every obstacle that comes our way.

Practicing Mindfulness and Meditation

In the chaotic and fast-paced world we live in, it's easy to become overwhelmed by the constant demands and challenges that life throws at us. Whether it's work-related stress, personal struggles, or simply trying to keep up with the ever-evolving society, we often find ourselves feeling exhausted, anxious, and disconnected. However, by incorporating the practices of mindfulness and meditation into our lives, we can find solace and regain control over our emotions and thoughts.

Mindfulness is the art of being fully present in the moment, without judgment or attachment. It allows us to become aware of our thoughts, emotions, and physical sensations, enabling us to respond to situations with clarity and compassion. By cultivating a mindful mindset, we can break free from the autopilot mode that often leads to stress and burnout.

Meditation, on the other hand, is a practice of training the mind to focus and redirect thoughts. It involves sitting quietly, observing the breath, and allowing thoughts to come and go without getting caught up in them. Through regular meditation, we can strengthen our ability to remain calm and centered, even in the face of adversity.

For all people, especially those caught in the relentless battle of life, incorporating mindfulness and meditation can be transformative. These practices offer a sanctuary amidst the chaos, allowing us to tap into our inner warrior and conquer life's challenges with grace and resilience.

When we practice mindfulness and meditation, we cultivate self-awareness and develop a deeper understanding of ourselves. We become more attuned to our thoughts, emotions, and physical sensations, enabling us to recognize and address any negative patterns or behaviors that may be hindering our growth. By becoming aware of our own struggles, we can better navigate through life's battles.

Mindfulness and meditation also provide us with a sense of inner peace and tranquility. As we learn to let go of worries and anxieties, we create space for joy, gratitude, and compassion to flourish within us. By nurturing a sense of inner peace, we become better equipped to handle the challenges that come our way.

In conclusion, the practices of mindfulness and meditation offer invaluable tools for all people, especially those engaged in the never-ending battle of life. By embracing these practices, we can unleash our inner warrior, mastering the art of conquering life's challenges with resilience, clarity, and compassion. So, take a moment, breathe, and step into the transformative journey of mindfulness and meditation – your inner warrior awaits.

Developing Emotional Intelligence

Subchapter: Developing Emotional Intelligence

In the battle of life, it is not just physical strength or intelligence that guarantees victory; it is the mastery of emotional intelligence. Emotional intelligence is the ability to understand, manage, and express our emotions effectively, and it plays a pivotal role in conquering life's challenges. Whether you are a young adult starting your career or a seasoned professional navigating complex relationship, developing emotional intelligence is essential for success and fulfillment in every aspect of life.

Emotional intelligence begins with self-awareness – the ability to recognize and understand our own emotions. This awareness allows us to identify our strengths, weaknesses, triggers, and values, enabling us to make better decisions and respond appropriately in tricky situations. By acknowledging our emotions without judgment, we can develop a deeper understanding of ourselves and our reactions, leading to greater personal growth and resilience.

Once we have mastered self-awareness, the next step is self-regulation. This involves managing our emotions, thoughts, and behaviors in a constructive manner. Instead of reacting impulsively or being controlled by our emotions, we can learn to pause, reflect, and choose our responses consciously. By developing self-control and adaptability, we become better equipped to handle the ups and downs of life, maintaining a calm and composed demeanor even in the face of adversity.

In addition to self-regulation, developing emotional intelligence also involves empathy – the ability to understand and consider the emotions of others. Empathy allows us to connect with people on a deeper level, fostering stronger relationships, effective communication, and collaboration. By putting ourselves in others' shoes, we can show compassion, offer support, and resolve conflicts more amicably. Developing empathy not only enhances our personal relationships but also improves our leadership skills, making us more effective in our professional lives.

To develop emotional intelligence, it is crucial to practice self-reflection, mindfulness, and active listening. By engaging in regular self-assessment and introspection, we can identify areas for improvement and work towards enhancing our emotional intelligence. Seeking feedback from trusted individuals and learning from their perspectives can provide valuable insights into our emotional blind spots.

Developing emotional intelligence is an ongoing journey that involves self-awareness, self-regulation, and empathy. By mastering these skills, we can navigate life's battles with greater resilience, understanding, and success. Whether you are facing personal challenges, professional setbacks, or trying to maintain healthy relationships, investing in emotional intelligence is the key to unleashing your inner warrior and conquering life's challenges with grace and wisdom.

Chapter 15: Strategies for Conquering Life's Challenges

Building a Supportive Network

In the battlefield of life, we often find ourselves facing numerous challenges that can seem overwhelming. Whether it's a personal struggle, a professional setback, or an emotional hurdle, we all need a support system to help us navigate these obstacles and emerge victorious. In this subchapter, we will explore the importance of building a supportive network and how it can empower us in conquering life's battles.

Regardless of our individual journeys, we cannot underestimate the power of surrounding ourselves with the right people. A staunch support network can provide encouragement, guidance, and a listening ear when we need it the most. These individuals can be our friends, family members, mentors, or even fellow warriors who have faced similar battles. They understand our struggles, empathize with our pain, and offer invaluable insights that can help us overcome any challenge.

One key aspect of building a supportive network is cultivating meaningful relationships. It's not just about having a large number of acquaintances, but rather about developing deep connections with those who genuinely care about our well-being. These genuine relationships are built on trust, respect, and mutual support. By investing time and effort into nurturing these connections, we create a solid foundation upon which we can lean during tough times.

Another crucial element of a supportive network is diversity. Surrounding ourselves with people from diverse backgrounds, experiences, and perspectives expands our horizons and equips us with a broader range of insights. This diversity can challenge our thinking, provide alternative solutions, and expose us to opportunities we may have never considered. By embracing diversity within our network, we not only gain valuable knowledge, but we also foster a sense of inclusivity and understanding in our own lives.

Furthermore, building a supportive network also involves being a supportive member of others' networks. It's a two-way street – just as we seek help and guidance, we must also be willing to offer it to others. By being a source of strength and encouragement for those around us, we create a reciprocal environment that uplifts everyone involved. This act of giving not only benefits others, but it also enhances our own growth and resilience as warriors in the battle of life.

Building a supportive network is paramount in conquering life's challenges. It provides us with the strength, inspiration, and guidance we need to overcome any obstacle that comes our way. By cultivating meaningful relationships, embracing diversity, and being a source of support for others, we create a powerful network that empowers us to unleash our inner warrior and master the art of conquering life's battles. Remember, you are not alone – together, we can conquer anything.

Seeking Opportunities for Growth

In the battle of life, we all face challenges that test our strength, resilience, and determination. It is during these trying times that we often find ourselves questioning our abilities and feeling overwhelmed. However, it is important to remember that within every challenge lies an opportunity for growth. In this subchapter, we will explore the significance of seeking opportunities for growth, regardless of the niche of "THE LIFE BATTLE."

Life's challenges come in various forms - be it personal, professional, or even emotional. While it may be easier to shy away from these challenges, it is essential to embrace them as opportunities for personal development. Seeking opportunities for growth requires a mindset shift, a willingness to step outside of our comfort zones, and a commitment to self-improvement.

One of the first steps in seeking opportunities for growth is to adopt a positive mindset. Instead of viewing challenges as roadblocks, we should see them as stepping stones towards personal growth. By reframing our perspective, we can shift our focus from the difficulties we face to the potential lessons and skills we can gain from overcoming them.

Furthermore, seeking opportunities for growth requires us to step outside of our comfort zones. Growth rarely occurs within the confines of familiarity. It is when we push ourselves beyond our limits, try new things, and take risks that we truly discover our capabilities. By embracing discomfort and embracing the unknown, we open ourselves up to a world of possibilities and personal growth.

Seeking opportunities for growth involves a commitment to self-improvement. This commitment requires actively seeking out challenges and continuously learning from them. Whether it is through reading books, attending seminars, or seeking mentorship, the key is to never stop growing. By investing in our personal and professional development, we equip ourselves with the tools needed to conquer life's challenges and emerge stronger than ever before.

To all people facing "THE LIFE BATTLE," remember that seeking opportunities for growth is a powerful weapon in your arsenal. Embrace the challenges you face, adopt a positive mindset, step outside of your comfort zone, and commit to self-improvement. Through this mindset and approach, you will not only conquer life's challenges but also emerge as a stronger, wiser, and more resilient individual.

In the battle of life, growth is not a luxury, but a necessity. Embrace it, seek it, and unleash your inner warrior to master the art of conquering life's challenges.

Embracing Failure and Learning from Mistakes

Failure is an inevitable part of life. It is the stepping stone to success and an essential part of personal growth. In the battle of life, we are bound to encounter setbacks and obstacles that can make us feel defeated. However, it is in these moments of failure that we have a tremendous opportunity for growth and learning.

Embracing failure means accepting that it is a natural part of the journey towards success. Instead of letting failure discourage us, we must use it as a valuable teacher. Every mistake we make provides us with an opportunity to learn, improve, and become better versions of ourselves.

One of the most significant obstacles to embracing failure is the fear of judgment and criticism from others. We often worry about what people will think if we fail or make mistakes. However, it is crucial to remember that everyone makes mistakes. In fact, some of the most successful individuals in history have experienced numerous failures before achieving greatness. By accepting failure as a part of life, we can let go of the fear of judgment and focus on learning from our mistakes.

Learning from our mistakes requires self-reflection and a willingness to accept responsibility. Rather than blaming external factors for our failures, we must take ownership of our actions and decisions. By doing so, we can identify the lessons that failure has to offer and make the necessary adjustments to improve ourselves.

In the battle of life, setbacks and failures can be discouraging. However, it is important to remember that failure is not the end, but merely a stepping stone towards success. Each failure brings us closer to our goals by providing valuable insights and lessons.

To truly embrace failure, we must cultivate a growth mindset. This means viewing failures as opportunities for growth and improvement rather than as personal shortcomings. By reframing our perspective, we can turn failures into motivations that propel us forward.

Embracing failure and learning from mistakes is crucial in our journey to conquer life's challenges. By accepting failure as a natural part of life, we can let go of the fear of judgment and focus on learning and growing from our mistakes. Each failure brings us closer to success by providing valuable lessons and insights. So, let us embrace failure, learn from our mistakes, and unleash our inner warriors to conquer life's battles.

Chapter 16: Thriving in Your Personal and Professional Life

Balancing Work and Personal Life

In today's fast-paced and demanding world, finding the right balance between work and personal life has become a challenge for many individuals. The constant juggling act between meeting professional obligations and nurturing personal relationships can often leave us feeling overwhelmed and drained. However, it is crucial to establish a harmonious equilibrium between these two crucial aspects of our lives in order to lead a fulfilling and successful life battle.

Work occupies a huge portion of our time and energy, providing us with financial stability and personal growth. However, it is important not to let work overshadow our personal lives, as neglecting our relationships, health, and passions can lead to a sense of emptiness and burnout. Therefore, it becomes imperative to prioritize and manage our time effectively.

One effective strategy for achieving a work-life balance is setting clear boundaries. This involves setting up defined working hours and sticking to them, allowing ourselves to disconnect from work and dedicate quality time to our personal lives. By doing so, we can ensure that we are fully present and engaged in our relationships and activities outside of work.

Another essential element in achieving a healthy balance is learning to delegate and ask for support when needed. Trying to handle all responsibilities alone can lead to stress and exhaustion. By delegating tasks at work and seeking help from family, friends, or professionals, we can lighten our workload and create more time for personal pursuits.

Self-care is a crucial part of maintaining a work-life balance. Taking care of our physical, mental, and emotional well-being is essential for our overall happiness and productivity. Engaging in activities that bring us joy and relaxation, such as exercise, hobbies, or spending time in nature, allows us to recharge and replenish our energy levels.

Additionally, effective communication is vital in striking the right balance. Clearly expressing our needs and expectations to both our professional and personal circles can help establish boundaries and prevent unnecessary conflicts. Open and honest communication ensures that our commitments are understood and respected by all parties involved.

Achieving a work-life balance is a constant endeavor that requires conscious effort and prioritization. By setting boundaries, delegating tasks, practicing self-care, and communicating effectively, we can create a harmonious blend of work and personal life. Remember, finding balance is not a one-size-fits-all solution; it is a personalized journey that requires continuous evaluation and adjustment. So, unleash your inner warrior and master the art of conquering life's challenges by striking a balance between work and personal life.

Building Healthy Relationships

In life, we are constantly faced with challenges, and one of the most critical battles we must conquer is building healthy relationships. Whether it's with our family, friends, or romantic partners, the quality of our relationships can greatly impact our overall well-being and happiness. In this subchapter, we will explore the key principles and strategies to cultivate and nurture healthy relationships, enabling us to conquer the battles that arise in our lives.

Primarily, communication is the foundation of any successful relationship. It is essential to express our thoughts, feelings, and needs openly and honestly, while also actively listening to others. Effective communication fosters understanding, resolves conflicts, and builds trust – all crucial elements for a healthy connection.

Another key aspect of building healthy relationships is practicing empathy and compassion. We must strive to understand and relate to the experiences and emotions of those around us. By putting ourselves in others' shoes, we can develop a deeper understanding and forge more meaningful connections.

Setting and respecting boundaries is vital for maintaining healthy relationships. Each person has their own limits and needs, and it is crucial to establish and communicate with them clearly. By respecting boundaries, we create a safe and comfortable environment that allows relationships to flourish.

Forgiveness is also a cornerstone of healthy relationships. We are all bound to make mistakes, and holding onto grudges only hinders our ability to grow together. Learning to forgive not only strengthens our relationships but also promotes personal growth and healing.

Additionally, investing time and effort into building healthy relationships requires patience and commitment. Relationships, like any worthy endeavor, require nurturing and continuous effort. By dedicating time and energy to our relationships, we create a solid foundation for lifelong connections.

It is important to surround ourselves with positive influences and avoid toxic relationships. Toxic relationships drain our energy, hinder personal growth, and hinder our ability to conquer life's battles. By consciously choosing to surround ourselves with individuals who uplift and support us, we create a positive and empowering environment that fuels our personal growth and resilience.

Building healthy relationships is a fundamental battle we must conquer in life. By prioritizing effective communication, empathy, setting boundaries, forgiveness, dedication, and surrounding ourselves with positive influences, we create a durable foundation for lifelong connections. Remember, the quality of our relationships greatly impacts our overall well-being, happiness, and ability to conquer life's challenges.

Achieving Success and Fulfillment

Success and fulfillment are two concepts that are deeply intertwined, yet often misunderstood. In our journey through life, we all strive to achieve these elusive goals, but the path to attaining them can be filled with obstacles and challenges. This subchapter aims to provide you with the necessary tools and mindset to conquer life's battles and unlock your true potential.

The first step towards achieving success and fulfillment is to define what these terms mean to you personally. Success can be measured in numerous ways - whether it's financial stability, professional accomplishments, or personal growth. Fulfillment, on the other hand, is often associated with a sense of purpose and contentment in one's life. By understanding your unique definition of success and fulfillment, you can align your efforts towards attaining them.

One crucial aspect of conquering life's battles is the development of a resilient mindset. Life is filled with difficulties, and setbacks are inevitable. However, it is how we respond to these challenges that truly defines our character. Embracing a warrior mentality allows us to face adversity head-on, learning from failures, and emerging stronger than before. It is essential to cultivate a positive mindset, focusing on solutions rather than dwelling on problems.

Another key element in achieving success and fulfillment is setting clear goals. Without a clear direction, we may find ourselves aimlessly wandering through life. By setting specific, measurable, achievable, relevant, and time-bound (SMART) goals, we can create a roadmap towards our desired outcomes. These goals act as a compass, guiding us through life's battles and empowering us to make focused and intentional decisions.

In addition to setting goals, it is vital to take consistent action towards their attainment. Success and fulfillment do not happen overnight; they are the result of persistent effort and dedication. By breaking down your goals into smaller, manageable tasks, you can make progress each day and stay motivated along the way. Remember, even the smallest steps can lead to significant achievements.

Lastly, success and fulfillment are not solely individual pursuits. Surrounding yourself with a supportive network of like-minded individuals can amplify your efforts and provide invaluable guidance and encouragement. Seek out mentors, join communities, and build relationships with those who share your aspirations. Together, you can navigate the challenges of life and celebrate each other's successes.

Achieving success and fulfillment is a lifelong journey that requires self-reflection, resilience, goal setting, consistent action, and a supportive network. By embracing the warrior within you, you can conquer life's battles and unlock your true potential. Remember, success and fulfillment are not destinations; they are the result of embracing the challenges and joys that life presents. Start your journey today and unleash your inner warrior.

Chapter 17: Unleashing Your Inner Warrior: Real-Life Stories of Triumph

Inspiring Stories of Overcoming Challenges

One who has conquered seemingly insurmountable challenges. These stories exemplify the indomitable human spirit and serve as a source of motivation for anyone navigating their own difficult journey.

From tales of overcoming physical disabilities to stories of triumph over mental health battles, these narratives demonstrate the power of perseverance, determination, and self-belief. Each story is a testament to the fact that no challenge is too great to overcome with the right mindset and determination.

You will read about individuals who defied the odds and turned their adversities into opportunities for growth and success. These individuals refused to let their circumstances define them and instead used their challenges as catalysts for personal transformation. By embracing their inner warrior, they were able to rise above their circumstances and emerge stronger than ever before.

Through these inspiring stories, readers will gain a deeper understanding of the human capacity for resilience and the potential within each of us to conquer life's toughest battles. The narratives provide valuable insights, practical tips, and actionable strategies for facing challenges head-on, fostering personal growth, and unleashing the inner warrior within.

Whether you are facing a physical, mental, emotional, or spiritual battle, these stories will remind you that you are not alone. They will ignite a fire within you, encouraging you to tap into your inner strength and unleash your true potential.

Prepare to be inspired, motivated, and empowered as you delve into the inspiring stories of those who have triumphed over adversity. Remember, the challenges we encounter in life are not meant to break us but to shape us into the warriors we are destined to become.

Lessons Learned from Warrior Mentors

In the journey of life, we all face various battles. Some may be external, such as financial struggles or career challenges, while others may be internal, such as self-doubt or emotional turmoil. No matter the nature of the battle, it is essential to equip ourselves with the right mindset and tools to conquer these challenges and emerge victorious. One invaluable resource we can tap into is the wisdom of warrior mentors who have triumphed over their own life battles.

Warrior mentors are individuals who have faced extraordinary circumstances and have emerged stronger and wiser. They have honed their skills, developed resilience, and possess a wealth of knowledge and experiences that can inspire and guide us through our own battles. By learning from their journeys, we can avoid the same pitfalls, gain valuable insights, and navigate our own paths more effectively.

One crucial lesson we can learn from warrior mentors is the power of perseverance. They teach us that giving up is not an option, even in the face of seemingly insurmountable obstacles. Their stories remind us that every battle is an opportunity for growth and that true strength lies in the ability to keep pushing forward, no matter how challenging the circumstances.

Another important lesson is the necessity of self-belief. Warrior mentors understand that success begins with a strong belief in oneself. They teach us to cultivate a mindset of confidence and resilience, to trust our abilities, and to never underestimate our potential. By developing an unshakable belief in ourselves, we can overcome any obstacle that life throws our way.

Warrior mentors also remind us of the significance of discipline and preparation. They emphasize the importance of training our minds and bodies to be at their best, enabling us to perform at optimal levels during life's battles. They teach us that success is not just about talent or luck but about consistent effort, practice, and preparation.

Furthermore, warrior mentors inspire us to embrace failure as a stepping stone to success. They share stories of their own setbacks and teach us that failure is not a reflection of our worth but an opportunity to learn, grow, and improve. By reframing failure as a valuable lesson, we can extract wisdom from every experience and use it to propel ourselves forward.

The lessons learned from warrior mentors are invaluable in our quest to conquer life's battles. By embracing the power of perseverance, self-belief, discipline, and learning from failure, we can unleash our inner warriors and master the art of conquering life's challenges. Let their wisdom guide us as we navigate our own battles and emerge stronger, wiser, and victorious.

Applying the Warrior Principles in Everyday Life

Life is often referred to as a battle, and we all face our fair share of challenges and obstacles along the way. Whether it's dealing with personal hardships, professional setbacks, or even finding the motivation to pursue our dreams, every day presents us with an opportunity to unleash our inner warrior and conquer life's challenges.

In the book "Unleashing Your Inner Warrior: Mastering the Art of Conquering Life's Challenges," we delve into the principles and techniques that can help all people, regardless of their background or current situation, overcome adversity and thrive in their everyday lives. This subchapter, titled "Applying the Warrior Principles in Everyday Life," serves as a practical guide for readers to implement these principles into their daily routines.

One of the fundamental principles we explore is the importance of mental resilience. Warriors are trained to develop a strong mindset that allows them to face any situation with courage and determination. By applying this principle in our own lives, we can learn to embrace challenges as opportunities for growth, rather than viewing them as insurmountable obstacles. We discuss techniques such as visualization, positive self-talk, and mindfulness that can help cultivate mental resilience and allow us to navigate through life's battles with grace and confidence.

Another key aspect we address is the role of discipline and self-mastery. Warriors are known for their unwavering commitment to their goals and their ability to stay focused even in the face of distractions. Applying this principle in our own lives means developing healthy habits and routines that support our growth and success. We explore techniques such as goal setting, time management, and self-reflection that can help readers establish a strong foundation for personal and professional achievement.

We emphasize the importance of physical well-being in conquering life's challenges. Warriors understand the importance of taking care of their bodies, as physical strength and vitality are crucial in any battle. By incorporating principles of proper nutrition, regular exercise, and self-care, readers can enhance their physical well-being and increase their overall resilience and energy levels.

"Applying the Warrior Principles in Everyday Life" is a subchapter that provides readers with practical tools and techniques to overcome life's battles. By embracing mental resilience, discipline, and physical well-being, all people can unleash their inner warrior and conquer any challenge that comes their way. Remember, life is a battle, but with the right mindset and strategies, we can emerge victorious and create the life we truly desire.

Chapter 18: Conclusion: Becoming the Master of Your Destiny

Embracing Your Inner Warrior

Life can often be described as a battle - a continuous struggle filled with obstacles and challenges that test our strength and resilience. In the face of these trials, it is essential to tap into the power within us and unleash our inner warrior. In the subchapter titled "Embracing Your Inner Warrior" from the book "Unleashing Your Inner Warrior: Mastering the Art of Conquering Life's Challenges," we delve into the depths of the human spirit and explore how we can harness its tremendous potential.

To all people facing the battles of life, this subchapter is a guiding light that illuminates the path towards personal growth, resilience, and triumph. Regardless of your background, age, or circumstances, the message remains the same - you have an inner warrior waiting to be unleashed.

The Life Battle is a battlefield where we encounter setbacks, disappointments, and hardships. It is during these times that our inner warrior awakens, ready to face the challenges head-on. Embracing your inner warrior begins with cultivating a mindset of strength, determination, and perseverance. It requires acknowledging your abilities, accepting your vulnerabilities, and finding the courage to overcome.

In this subchapter, we explore various techniques and strategies to connect with your inner warrior. We delve into the power of positive affirmations, visualization, and self-belief. We invite you to uncover the warrior within through meditation and mindfulness practices that foster self-awareness and inner peace. Additionally, we provide practical tips on how to build resilience, maintain motivation, and develop a growth mindset that enables you to thrive in the face of adversity.

Embracing your inner warrior is not about suppressing emotions or denying vulnerability. On the contrary, it is about embracing your authenticity and finding strength in your vulnerability. It is through the acknowledgment of our fears and insecurities that we can tap into the wellspring of courage and determination within us.

"Embracing Your Inner Warrior" is a subchapter that encourages all people facing life's battles to awaken their latent strength and resilience. It serves as a guide to help you navigate the challenges of life and appear victorious. By tapping into your inner warrior, you will discover a power within you that can conquer any obstacle and achieve your dreams. Remember, you are stronger than you think, and your inner warrior is eagerly waiting to be unleashed.

Taking Action and Conquering Life's Challenges

Life is a battlefield, and every day we face different challenges that test our resilience, determination, and inner strength. It is during these moments of adversity that we have the opportunity to unleash our inner warrior and conquer whatever life throws at us. In this subchapter, we will explore the strategies and mindset needed to take action and overcome life's challenges, regardless of the circumstances.

The first step towards conquering life's challenges is to acknowledge and embrace them. It is essential to face the reality of the situation and understand that challenges are a natural part of life. By accepting this truth, we can shift our perspective from being a victim to becoming a warrior ready to take on any obstacle.

Once we have accepted the challenge, it is time to formulate a plan of action. This involves breaking down the problem into smaller, manageable steps. By doing so, we can approach the challenge with clarity and focus, making it easier to tackle. Remember, a warrior does not run blindly into battle but strategizes and plans their moves carefully.

Taking action requires courage and determination. It is crucial to push through fear and self-doubt, knowing that the only way to conquer a challenge is to face it head-on. As warriors, we must be willing to step out of our comfort zones and embrace discomfort, for it is in discomfort that we grow and find true strength.

In the face of adversity, it is also important to cultivate a positive mindset. By focusing on the possibilities and opportunities that arise from challenges, we can transform them into catalysts for personal growth. A warrior sees challenges as opportunities for self-improvement and uses them to build resilience and character.

Furthermore, seeking support and guidance from others can greatly enhance our ability to conquer life's challenges. Surrounding ourselves with a dedicated support network of like-minded individuals or seeking professional help can offer valuable insights, encouragement, and accountability during tough times.

Finally, it is crucial to celebrate every victory, no matter how small. By acknowledging our progress and accomplishments, we reinforce our belief in ourselves and our ability to overcome anything life throws our way.

Taking action and conquering life's challenges requires a warrior's mindset, courage, determination, and a positive outlook. By embracing challenges, formulating a plan, taking action, seeking support, and celebrating victories, we can unleash our inner warrior and master the art of conquering life's challenges. Remember, you are capable of far more than you can imagine, and with the right mindset and strategies, you can triumph over any battle life presents.

Living a Purposeful and Fulfilled Life

In the battle of life, it is essential to not only survive but to thrive. To navigate through the challenges and obstacles that come our way, we must tap into our inner warrior and unleash our potential. The key to conquering life's challenges lies in living a purposeful and fulfilled life.

Living a purposeful life means having a clear sense of direction and aligning our actions with our values and goals. It is about discovering our passions and talents and using them to make a positive impact in the world. When we live with purpose, we find meaning in our everyday actions, and this gives us the motivation and drive to overcome any obstacle that comes our way.

To live a purposeful life, it is crucial to define our personal mission statement. This is a statement that encapsulates our core values, passions, and goals. It serves as a compass that guides our decisions and actions. By having a clear mission statement, we can make choices that align with our purpose and avoid getting caught up in the distractions and temptations that may lead us astray.

Fulfillment, on the other hand, comes from living in alignment with our purpose. It is about finding joy and satisfaction in what we do and being true to ourselves. When we live a fulfilled life, we experience a deep sense of contentment and happiness. It is not about external accomplishments or material possessions but rather about living authentically and embracing the journey.

To live a purposeful and fulfilled life, we must cultivate self-awareness and continuously evaluate our actions and choices. We need to ask ourselves if our current path aligns with our purpose and if it brings us fulfillment. If not, it is essential to make adjustments and course corrections to stay true to our inner warrior's calling.

Living a purposeful and fulfilled life requires courage and resilience. We must be willing to take risks, face our fears, and learn from our failures. It is through overcoming challenges that we grow and evolve, and it is in the face of adversity that our inner warrior shines the brightest.

Living a purposeful and fulfilled life is the key to conquering life's battles. By aligning our actions with our purpose and finding fulfillment in our journey, we can navigate through challenges and obstacles with resilience and grace. Let us unleash our inner warrior and master the art of living a purposeful and fulfilled life.

Thank you for taking the time to read my book. All my books are written from my life experiences. I always tell others to NEVER QUIT. We have incredible minds; with them we can do ANYTHING! Find my other books at all book retailers and online.

Kevin

'LIFE WARRIOR'